blanky

kealan patrick
burke

ISBN: 1977550444
ISBN-13: 978-1977550446

"Everyone can master a grief but he that has it."
 - William Shakespeare, *Much Ado About Nothing*

* * *

YOU SAY YOU CAN'T IMAGINE what it must be like to lose a child.

Let me make it easy for you.

It's the beginning of the end of your world.

Imagine the thing that means most to you being erased from your life. For me, it was Robin, my daughter. She was just a baby not even old enough to have fully developed into a regular human being. She had no real personality yet. She just ate, shat, and slept. Sometimes she cooed, sometimes she gurgled, sometimes she laughed. She smelled faintly of milk and baby powder. I loved her. She was the most special thing in the world, even when I had to be at work at eight and she woke me up at six for her bottle, or to be changed. Even when the long periods of late-night shrieking threatened to drive me to anger. Even when I didn't know how to calm her down and my head started hurting so bad I thought I would join her in crying.

I loved her.

One rainy night I put her to bed and when I woke up, she was dead.

That was the beginning of the end of my world.

This is the rest of it.

1

IT ONLY TOOK ME FORTY YEARS TO LEARN how to sew buttons back on a coat, and only the death of my daughter to realize it was something that needed doing. Without those buttons, the eyeholes would widen, the material would fray, and the coat would sunder on its hanger like a vampire exposed to sunlight. And once that happened, what was to keep the same from happening to me? I often felt like that early on, like I was suspended from a hook in the dark just waiting to fall apart.

Thus, three months after Robin died, all the loose or missing buttons on my coats and jackets had been returned to their as-new firmness. In some cases, those buttons wouldn't budge at all, as if I'd glued them on. Inevitably this would cause me some difficulty, but I knew I'd simply tear them off just for the excuse to sew them back on. It was a ritual, one of the few that kept me grounded, no matter how silly it appeared on the surface.

On the day I found the blanket, I was alone, wandering around the house like a ghost.

Loneliness sent me to my cell phone and the still-not familiar procedure of dialing my wife's number for anything other than to ask what time she'd be home. But she wasn't coming home, and every day she was away, I felt the chances of reconciliation growing slimmer. Soon she would become, like our lost daughter, a memory confined to a frame or my own fevered dreaming. They would exist only to hurt by virtue of their maddening unattainability.

The connection hummed and I imagined the signal shooting across the miles between us, flung between towers, fired down through the phalanxes of knotted trees, over the stone walls around her parent's house, and on into the steel, plastic, and glass handset, her phone's display showing a picture of me smiling in a way I suspected I never would again: carefree, loved, alive. Above that picture, instead of "HUBBY", it probably just read "STEPHEN."

I wondered if this was one of the days in which she felt compelled to answer, and was relieved when the dial tone ended and her voice came on the line, immediately bringing butterflies to my stomach.

"Hey," Lexi said.

"Hey. How are you?"

Is there a more redundant question to ask a grieving person? *How are you? Still moping around because the most precious thing in your life got erased? Still struggling with suicidal thoughts quite simply because you'd rather be dead than live without your baby daughter?*

"Oh, you know," she said, because I do. What I didn't know was why I'd called in the first place, or what was left to say between us, but it seemed critical to not let the silence get too thick for fear we'd drown in it.

"How are your folks?" I asked.

"Pretty good, considering. They say hi."

Given that my relationship with her parents had never been optimal, I doubted that very much, but it was good of her to say it. "Tell them I say hi, too."

"How are *you* holding up?"

"Okay, I suppose. I miss you."

She didn't respond. I knew she wouldn't, hoped she would.

"Any chance I could talk you into stopping by, just to...you know...talk?"

"I'm not sure I'm ready for that, Stephen."

Do you ever stop to consider how seldom your significant other uses your name in daily life? For us it was always some term of endearment, like "honey" or "babe", or even the more extravagant "sugar badger" or "manly mouse". The only time that changed was during arguments when the strangeness of being called by your name left no doubt that you were in trouble.

"Would you think about it, at least?"

It took her a long time to reply. "Sure."

3

"It's just that I feel lost in this house without you."

"I'm surprised you're still there," she said, with just the faintest hint of bitterness, the unspoken implication being that I should have fled the scene like she had, but unlike Lexi, I had no place else to go.

"This is home, Lex. *Our* home."

"No, it isn't. It's the house where our daughter died, and that's all it can ever be."

"Don't say that. We can—"

"Look, I'm not going to have this conversation with you right now."

"Or ever."

"What?"

"Nothing. Just talk to me, would you? Just for a little while?"

"I have to go."

"Babe..."

"Take care, Stephen, okay?"

Stephen. I might as well have been one of her coworkers from the office calling to follow up on a monthly expense report.

"Lex."

And then it was just me sitting on the sofa alone, the phone in my hands and tears in my eyes, the yellow-painted walls robbed of their color by the lack of light through the curtained windows. The only sound in the world was the thunder of my heartbeat in my ears. My hands were shaking, so I clasped them together and clenched my teeth against the black wall of grief that rose behind my eyes. This could not be all there was. It couldn't be the end. I needed light. I needed hope. I needed help, but there was nobody to call. It had always been just me and Lex and, for a little while, Robin, and now they were gone and I was alone.

But there was no time for self-pity.

Through blurry eyes, I checked the time on my phone. The day was not yet done, and neither was I. Resolute, yet shaken, I stood and went to the closet, donned my coat with its snugly repaired buttons, and stormed out into the bright fall afternoon, my intent to walk off the ennui of isolation, the fear of the life in which I had abruptly found myself. After all, if I could fix an old coat, then surely, I could find a way to sew myself back together.

* * *

I walked the rain-slicked streets with false purpose, my sure stride a ploy meant to fool myself into thinking I had anywhere to go. When you're circling the drain, worrying about direction is pointless. So, I plodded on, my eyes on the cobblestone walkways glistening grayly beneath a vibrant veneer of dead leaves. Cars sizzled through puddles. Dark figures hustled by, unburdened by the absence of a destination, all elbows and impatience. I was a ghost in the glass storefronts, fading as the day grew old. Fat pumpkins on stoops watched my passage with hollow-eyed glee. Time would shrink them too.

At length, I realized my path had been predetermined after all. The sky, a charcoal palette of swirling clouds and streaks of muted light, cast a pall on the cross-studded mounds of green before me. The entrance to the graveyard—a tall stone arch bearing Latin words I did not understand—was appropriately Gothic, as was the wrought iron fence meant to keep out those for whom burial sites held some strange and not always benevolent nocturnal attraction.

For the longest time, long enough for my own shadow to distance itself from me, I stared at that gate as if it was some mystical portal to a realm I couldn't possibly understand, but the only thing that baffled me was the reality that, no matter how indirectly, I had put someone here. Inside, buried six feet in the dirt, were the tiny bones of my daughter, a new life extinguished and hidden in the earth. My baby. Robin. Here and then gone forever.

As the tears welled and the strength threatened to leave my legs, an old lady, her bones and expression mercilessly twisted by age and a life hard-lived, sidled out from behind the gate and squinted up at me, her left eye lost in folds of wrinkles, the other opaque and watering from the cold. She wore a headscarf and coat in seasonal colors of yellow and red. "He left me a decade ago," she said with a faint smile as she drew abreast of me. Her words were smoky, like the breeze. "Went to lay with the Goddess of Grief, like we all do in the end." She raised a hand, waggled her gnarled fingers in farewell, and shambled on.

Some unmeasured time later, still held in thrall by the stone arch and those Latin letters, I decided that today, clearly, I was not up to the task of entering the graveyard, not prepared to kneel by my daughter's grave with its small polished headstone and repeat apologies for the breeze to whip away from my lips. I was already living in the house where our worst nightmares had come true. That day, I could not push myself to revisit the place where that nightmare had left her. And so, I went home, and took a different route than before to make it feel as if I had accomplished something, but around every corner, hidden in the shadows between the houses, and in the windows where my pale face hovered like a Halloween mask, all I could see was my wife's screaming face as she held our lifeless daughter in her arms. And with it, came the memory, the treasured and accursed memory I come back to so very often of that one blissful moment in which I didn't know Robin was dead. The pre-moment ignorance in which I could have lived forever if it meant I'd never have to know the truth. But then the stark reality struck me at the look on Lexi's face, at the sound of her horrified, anguished scream, a sound I had never heard her make before. Then I saw Robin's tiny little hand, and realized it was the wrong color, and everything grew dim.

* * *

Mail awaited me on my return: overdue notices, mostly, and my paycheck, which could not hope to cover them. Death is expensive, and like grief, is not likely to go away without being dealt with directly and at length. But not today. I tossed the envelopes on the table by the front door, hung up my coat, then poured myself a generous measure of whiskey. Humming some tune I couldn't identify under oath, I planted myself on the sofa before the TV. I had come to think of old sitcoms like *Cheers*, *WKRP in Cincinnati*, and *M*A*S*H* as a kind of therapy, isolating me from the isolation, if you will. I sat in the glow of the TV in a room empty but for me, the sofa, and the rug Lexi and I bought at an Indian reservation in New Mexico. (Only when we got home did we see the tag that said it was made in China.)

I was three whiskeys deep and chuckling robotically at McLean Stevenson's drunken attempts to seduce a nurse when I heard a sound from upstairs. It distracted me only mildly, worthy of notice not concern. The seasons were changing and the house was old, attuned like arthritic bones to alterations in temperature. I grew up in the house and knew its rhythms well, so I returned to the security of the world within the TV, let myself get recruited by the staff and soldiers at the 4077th and laughed at their shenanigans. It made little sense that I should wish I were there at a fictional mobile army surgical hospital during the Korean war, and yet it still seemed better than being here, if only because those folks had each other for solace, and knew how to find humor in the horror as a means of coping. This was not something I had been able to manage. Even when I laughed at the TV, the sound was hollow, an automatic response designed to keep me sane, but not loud enough to be persuasive.

Soon my glass was empty and I did not chastise myself for how unsteady I was when I rose to fetch another. This was, after all, the point. For a few hours at least, I would have some small semblance of respite from the dread that, in my waking hours, clung to me like a heavy coat.

From upstairs, another sound, this time a shifting, as of something being dragged across the floor. Empty glass in hand, I looked up, as if being tipsy now came with the bonus of being able to see through ceilings. Canned laughter filled the room, but now it was lost on me. Seemed inappropriate, incongruous. Horror movies would be a lot less effective if prerecorded laughter took the place of ominous music during the scary scenes. And make no mistake, I was scared now. The creaking of timbers settling, of joints tightening, that was familiar. A dragging sound was not. Up there, through that ceiling, was the floor of an empty room. But once upon a time, not so very long ago, it had been Robin's room.

7

I hadn't been inside that room in months for the same reason my wife hadn't been in this house for six weeks. The pain was much too potent here. Standing at the threshold of Robin's room, seeing where her crib used to be, only served to remind us of what could have been done had we known it was necessary. We did not deserve to be blamed for her death. On some level, my wife and I both knew this, and yet it was impossible not to hold ourselves accountable, to wish that we had just taken our baby to bed with us that night instead of leaving her to die alone in her crib. We were good parents, I doubt anyone would have argued against that, but still she died. Someone must bear the blame for that crippling reality no matter how illogical or unfair it may be. Lexi blamed me, and herself, in equal measure. And I guess if I'm being honest, I felt the same at first. We were, after all, the guardians tasked with Robin's well-being, and we failed, and now she was gone. And that was what I feared would build a permanent and impenetrable wall between us. Eventually she would move out for good and then move on with her life, and I wouldn't be in it. She'd remarry, maybe even have more children, but I feared that when Robin died, Lexi buried me right alongside her. For me, that doubled the grief, and in my darkest hours, tended a black flame of anger in my heart that Lexi should abandon me when she knew I needed her, knew that we should seek solace in each other if we were to have any hope of making it through this.

Or perhaps that was only what *I* needed.

That sound again.

Perhaps it was the whiskey or the anger that emboldened me, but with a shaky sigh, I set down my glass and headed upstairs. The fantastic notions of what might await me behind the locked door of that room were not difficult to dismiss, even in so vulnerable a state. I did not anticipate a visitation, a haunting, or some inexplicable occurrence attributable to the paranormal. I had never believed in such things, no matter how much I might have wished that I did, if only so I could have known Robin was in a better place and not just lying in cold dead earth forevermore. It would have been so much easier to believe in ghosts, but what I expected to find in that room was a natural visitor, most likely a squirrel. It wouldn't have been the first time they'd inveigled their way into the house in search of a warm place to build a nest, and the nature of the sound suggested them as the likely culprits.

Still, standing outside my daughter's door, I found myself paralyzed.

In the center of the four wooden panels on the white door, there was a single sticker: a cartoon ladybug with big round eyes and a comical smile. From that mouth jutted a speech balloon containing the words: "Oh, hai!" I had always found that little sticker adorable. Now I found it almost debilitatingly sad.

I have no idea how much time passed, how many rounds of canned laughter carried hollowly up the stairs with the TV casting lightning against the wall beside me, before the shuffling sound came again and I moved my head away from where I had been pressing it against the door.

I looked at the door knob, head cocked, listening.

The sound did not come again.

I was content to believe it had been nothing at all, imagination perhaps, or at least, something not worthy of investigation right at that very moment. And yet...

I opened the door.

2

IN THE WEEKS AFTER THE FUNERAL, we stripped Robin's room bare. Down came the curtains (pink with red hearts) and the matching lamp shade. Away went the fluffy pink rug. We put all Robin's toys and her mobile into black plastic bags and stowed them in the closet alongside the boxes of her clothes and the skeleton of the deconstructed crib. We broke down a lot that day, and every day after. I thought after the horror of finding Robin cold and unresponsive that awful Monday morning and then watching as her tiny coffin was lowered into the ground, that nothing could hurt me more. I was wrong. Erasing all trace of her from inside our home was just as bad. We justified it by telling ourselves that leaving everything where it was would ultimately do more harm than good by serving as a constant reminder, and yet systematically shoving everything into sacks and boxes and tossing them into the closet felt so much worse. Like we were being disrespectful of her memory. Like we didn't care, and now only wanted to get on with our lives. And to a certain degree, you *must* try to get on with things or the grief will destroy you. You *must* put away the reminders of loss to have any hope of surviving. And we did. We locked them all away, like you lock all the pain away in your heart and wait for time to build a shield around it.

All but the blanket in which we'd swaddled her while we waited for the paramedics. Only now did I realize I never knew what became of it. I guess I assumed it went with her to the hospital or was lost somewhere along the way in that long grim process between institutions of hope and the desolation of the grave.

Now, door open, my hand still on the knob and my lungs

shuddering with the strain of holding back the tears, I finally knew where that blanket had ended up.

It was sitting there before me on the floor of her room.

* * *

There was only a single window in that room, and with no curtains or the crib to obstruct it, the streetlamp outside cast a hazy oblong of yellow light on the hardwood floor. The blanket sat in this wedge of sickly light. All I could do was stare at it in sad wonder. Why was it there? *How* was it there? Even though it had been some time since I'd last entered the room, I knew without a doubt that the blanket had not been there on that occasion or any other following Robin's death. Assuming the sound I'd heard had been the blanket being displaced from its original location, who or what had moved it, and from where?

The answer when it came was obvious and unpleasant.

The squirrels. Invasive little fuckers must have tugged it free from wherever it had been stowed.

The closet door, however, was closed. I stepped inside the room and looked up. The two small vents in the ceiling were shut too, or at least shut enough to prevent rodents from infiltrating them. Still, despite no apparent means of ingress, I knew better than to assume there wasn't one. Squirrels are crafty bastards when they need to be and for all I knew, they were living beneath the floorboards and could spring up out of them whenever they saw fit. I made a note to call pest control on Monday, knowing I wouldn't do any such thing. It was merely a rational response to an irrational event.

Braced by a level of unease I couldn't accurately explain, I crossed the room and scooped up the blanket. When the material touched my fingers, I felt a jolt of discomfort that travelled like an electrical current up my arm into my chest and neck, and reflexively I let the blanket fall to the floor. Then I followed it down, landing hard on my knees, and brought a hand up to cover my mouth, as if worried someone might hear me choking on the tears.

In the square of light on the floor, that pale blue cotton blanket might as well have been a view into my daughter's open grave for all the sorrow it invoked. I wanted to touch it again, bring it to my face and smell it to see if it still had her scent, but I was afraid. Instead, I spent an hour just staring at the picture in the center of it, which depicted two rabbits dressed in Victorian clothes holding red balloons made of felt. They looked strangely sullen for something intended to comfort children, their clothes shabby and old. One rabbit was taller than the other. Their oversized eyes looked like ragged thumbprints, their mouths hanging open, tongues exposed, as if they were supposed to be speaking a message their creator forgot to add. Age had unraveled the embroidery in places, giving some of their limbs a palsied, unfinished look. The smaller of the two rabbits had free-floating hands, his wrists undone by wear. If anything, their postures and expressions indicated irritation, as if observing them was a form of intrusion. One couldn't help but feel as if they were originally intended to be looking at each other, not the viewer, and had ceased their discussion to chide me. There were three wavy lines of dashes beneath their feet to indicate the ground upon which they stood. It looked like furrowed earth, like farmland. It was an odd and not at all cheery illustration, which led me to wonder, for the first time, where and why Lexi bought it.

I wiped my eyes and rose, knees aching, and grabbed the blanket. This time, there was no jolt, though the material was cold against my skin, no doubt from lying on the floor.

Closing the door behind me, I left Robin's room and headed for the phone.

Despite my sorrow, despite the surprise at finding Robin's blanket, I was not drunk or foolish enough to squander the opportunity to use it as leverage.

* * *

It took four attempts to get Lexi to answer, but despite the late hour, I persisted, and at last, she picked up, her exasperation quickly giving way to interest at the mention of my discovery.

"Her blanket? Which one?"

"The one from her crib. The faded blue cotton one with the rabbits and balloons on it."

"Didn't we…? I thought we lost that."

"Me too."

"You said it was just lying on the floor?"

"Yes."

"How come you're only finding it now?"

"I don't—"

"That was her favorite blanky, remember?"

I resisted the tactless urge to point out that nine-month old children probably aren't developed enough or haven't lived long enough to prefer one thing over another, and waited for her to continue.

"Why would it be there though? We cleaned that room and put everything away."

"That was my thought."

"You don't think…?"

"I didn't think anything, to be honest. I just grabbed it and called you." The lie was meant to dissuade the notion I knew was forming in her head, the same one I'd resisted because it could only lead to more pain. *No, Lexi, I do not believe it's a sign.*

"I'd like to have it, Stephen. Would you mind?"

I looked down at the blanket spread across my lap, the blue so faded it was almost gray, one rabbit swollen across my knee, the other vanished in the fold between my legs. "Of course, babe. I can mail it to you, or drop it off on my way to—"

"No, that would take too long. Can I come over and get it tonight?"

I sat up, startled, blanket and fresh drink forgotten, and focused on the hairline crack in the living room wall. Committed as I'd been not to entertain false hope, in that moment it was hard not to acknowledge it capering in the background. "Sure, sure. When?"

"I could be there in an hour if you're staying up."

If I hadn't planned on being up late drinking anyway, I'd certain have amended my schedule to accommodate her. She hadn't stepped foot in this house in so long and even though I knew I should manage my expectations (she was, after all, coming for the blanket, not me), it was hard to deny the pulse of excitement at the prospect of her visit.

"I'll be up. Of course I will."

"Okay. Thank you, Stephen. I'll see you soon."

And then she was gone.

I took a few moments to let the hope war with reason before I realized the place was a mess. In a heartbeat, I was on my feet and flitting from room to room, clearing away the evidence of my enforced bachelordom. Then, with mere minutes to spare, I took a quick shower, brushed my teeth, and changed my clothes. By the time the doorbell rang, I was as presentable as I was going to get on such short notice.

* * *

Lexi, on the doorstep, her hair misted with rain. "Hey." Behind her, the waxy leaves on the succulents glistened in the dark and wept tears of their own. Her smile was frail, uncertain, her arms folded defensively against whatever negative (or perhaps even positive) responses I might have about her being there. I was careful not to rush her and smother her with kisses or wrap my arms around her and squeeze her so tight she'd never be able to leave again. Instead, I smiled and stepped back to let her in. It felt weird permitting her entry to a house we'd shared for six years, the house where we ate, slept, discussed everything under the sun, made love, became parents elated and then later, devastated. The house where we became *us*.

As she passed me in the hallway, the scent of her perfume set my nerves alight, and I shut the door on the night and the rain with my eyes closed, before following her into the living room.

The blanket was folded on the back of the sofa. Immediately she spotted it and picked it up. I watched her bring it to her face and breathe deep, her eyes shimmering with tears.

"God. It still smells like her."

"Do you…would you like a drink?"

14

She nodded silently and sat down on the sofa, the blanket folded on her lap. She stroked it as if it were a sleeping animal. "You didn't think it was strange that the blanket was just *there* for you to find?"

I measured her whiskey as carefully as my words. "I was just surprised. I hadn't been in there for a long time. Could be it fell from one of the boxes and we just didn't notice it on our way out."

I dropped two ice cubes into her drink and took both glasses out to the living room. I didn't wish to crowd her, so I sat on the armchair opposite and set our drinks down on the coffee table between us. She was still fawning over the blanket and paying me little mind.

"I don't remember where you bought that," I said, when the silence between us began to thicken.

A wistful smile brightened her pale face. "If it had been any other place, I probably wouldn't remember the name of it, but it wasn't. I got it at Columbus Market, remember? It was the Sunday right after we found out I was pregnant. You spent most of the time poring over the old paintings and first edition books. I was looking at decorations for the house. Then I saw that old man with the sign for baby clothes on his rickety little stall."

And with that, I remembered. "Only, he didn't spell it right."

Her smile broadened, fingers tracing the outlines of the pair of rabbits on the blanket. "He spelled it 'Baby Close.'"

"Yeah, I remember that now. The guy with the glass eye."

"He was so sweet to me."

She had yet to look away from the blanket. Instead, she continued to stroke it lovingly as if somehow that might make Robin appear from the material. Then, abruptly, her face collapsed and she burst into tears. I moved to her side so fast I knocked my drink over, and clumsily took her in my arms. At first, she resisted, her body stiff as a board, but then she relented and leaned into me, her face buried in my shirt as she sobbed, her fingers like claws grabbing at my shoulders as if she was trying to climb inside me for a place to hide. I held her tightly, my chin resting on the top of her head, and now it was impossible not to hope that this moment, this breakdown, our togetherness, might signal a willingness to tackle the grief as a unit instead of apart.

"Why did she have to die?" my wife asked, and for that I had no good answer, and nowhere to find one. What words did come were lost in my own tears, and then we were crying together, a shuddering, ugly mess of whispers, sighs, and sobs.

When at last we were as composed as we were going to get, we sought solace in the whiskey. Lament became celebration of the light Robin had brought to our lives for her brief stay with us.

"I'll never forget the first time she threw up on you."

I grimaced. "Jesus, the smell. It was like she'd been eating from the trashcan."

"I couldn't stop laughing."

"I know, I remember. I also remember wondering how on earth I was going to be able to deal with that every day until she was old enough to take over."

"And I remember worrying that you were going to keep trying to make excuses so you wouldn't have to."

More tears followed, then comfort, then laughter, and finally love. We held hands and sat close enough that I could feel the warmth of her through my clothes.

"I feel like I didn't even have a chance to know her," Lex said. "That she was this precious, beautiful little thing I was tasked with seeing through life and I couldn't keep her safe. What kind of a mother…what kind of a person does that make me?"

"Don't say that. You were a great mother. You doted on her. We both did. Horrible things happen every day. Losing her was just…the horrible thing that happened to us."

"I don't know what to do, Stephen. I really don't. Every day I'm alive seems like an insult to her memory. Why should I be allowed to go on when something so innocent was just casually snuffed out, for no reason at all? I still wake up every morning forgetting that she's gone, until the pain rushes in and it's so fresh and so sharp I want to die to escape it." She wiped her nose on her sleeve. "So many people keep saying they're sorry for my loss that I don't want to leave the house. It angers me. Even though I know it shouldn't, that they're just trying to be caring, decent people, it makes me mad. I want to ask them what they're sorry for, or how they can even pretend to be sorry when they don't know how it feels. It puts a brick wall up between us, and it's unfair because it makes me forget that everyone has lost someone, and nobody knows how to cope. I end up hating myself for hating the people who care."

I threaded my fingers through hers. "That's how I've felt, so many times. But we must go on, Lex. There might be a million reasons why we can't, or shouldn't, but we must, and that's all there is to it."

"I don't know *how*, though. Most of the time I don't even know why I should be allowed to."

"Me neither." I took a deep breath and slowly released it. "All I do know is that I don't want to do it alone. And weren't we always stronger together? We always said nothing would come between us, that there was nothing we couldn't conquer. I know at the time we never imagined in a million years it would be something *this* fucking apocalyptic, but still…I meant it then and I mean it now. We're stronger together than we'll ever be alone."

"I know, but…I see her in you, Stephen. She had your eyes, and it got so that looking at you felt like looking at her, and all I could see was the accusation, the blame. I couldn't bear it. I still can't."

I put my hand to her cheek and turned her head so that she was looking at me.

"Lex, she's at peace. Our little girl is at peace, and it's time you allowed yourself the same mercy, but you've got to let me help you, and you've got to help me too. I need your strength or I'll never make it through this."

Lex moved away and I felt dread in my chest that maybe that had been the wrong thing to say or the wrong time to say it.

For a long while she just stared at the blanket in her lap.

"Lex?"

"I love you," she said then, so low I feared I'd misheard, but then she kissed me so very softly, her fingers on my cheek, and asked if she could stay rather than risk a drunken drive home in the rain. I answered by leading her upstairs where we lost ourselves in each other for a time. It was a merciful, wonderful, blissful reprieve from the sorrow.

We fell asleep to the sound of a storm.

* * *

I awoke to sunshine streaming through a window still speckled with the previous night's rain. For a moment, I was unsure whether I'd dreamed the events of the night before. It would hardly have been the first time my subconscious had hoodwinked me with elaborate fantasies of a life less hostile than mine had become. The fear was not helped by the fact that I was alone in my bed. A quick check of my watch showed that it was almost noon, which meant I was four hours late for work. Not that they'd mind. Principal Lewis seemed to understand that my attendance on any given day was directly proportional to my emotional state, and that maybe being faced by a bunch of children wasn't the best thing for me at the time. I'm not entirely sure he was right about that. I loved my students and maybe seeing them might have helped. I don't know, but I was quite happy to take advantage of his assumptions to the contrary.

I hurried downstairs, head pounding from an incumbent hangover I was too alarmed to fully acknowledge.

Robin's blanket—*Blanky*—was gone.

So was Lexi.

But any disappointment I might have felt was dispelled by the note she'd left for me on the kitchen counter.

It read:

Thank you for being there for me last night. I felt more human than I have in months. And I'm sorry I've been so distant. I think I forgot how good you've always been for me, and I shouldn't have shut you out. I'm not going to make unreasonable promises to you. Not yet. There's a lot of ground still to cover, but call me when you wake up. We have a lot to discuss.

Love,

Lex

P.S. I stole a bagel.

There was much to register about that note, all of it good. For the moment, as I released a breath that felt as if it had been trapped in dusty lungs since the day Lex left to go stay with her parents, I chose only to focus on a single word from the letter: *Love.*

I brewed myself a cup of coffee and scooped up the phone. Dialing my wife's number, I was astonished and gratified to find that I was smiling. It seemed totally inappropriate, absolutely alien, and immeasurably good.

She answered on the first ring.

THE WALL BETWEEN US DID NOT COME DOWN overnight, nor did we expect it to. It was heartening enough to know that the will was there, and thus we were content to remove one brick at a time. Lexi did not move back in with me, though it was discussed as an eventuality, and while disappointed, I deferred to her wish to maintain a little distance.

"It's just easier to think, being away from there, easier to heal."

I understood, of course. She needed to build up the strength to be able to face the house in which she'd endured the worst thing that had ever happened to her, even though my own suffering would have been greatly allayed by her presence. But I could wait. I would wait, for as long as it took. It was enough to feel her love again, to feel that wall crumbling down.

Over the next few weeks, we met for coffee, went for walks, went to the movies. Afterward, she'd come home with me and we would make slow, passionate love until the sun rose, and then, whenever possible, stay in bed together all day, just talking and holding each other. On one of these days, we ordered pizza and wings and messed up the sheets and each other, which led to us sharing a shower, something I don't think we'd done since our early dating days. It didn't kill the pain—nothing but time would do that, and even then, not completely—but it was a wonderful reprieve from its sharpest edges.

Eventually, she returned to her parents' house, and I returned to work.

The kids in my class were overjoyed to have me back, though whether or not this was because the substitute teacher was a battleaxe, I can't say. They asked a lot of questions I wasn't really prepared to answer, so I distracted them by allowing them reading time rather than burden them with instruction. The staff, too, seemed inordinately happy to see me. Apparently, rumors had started to circulate that I might never be coming back. I found their concern touching and sincere, especially since I'd never considered any of them close, and thus, I accepted their invitation to attend the regular Friday karaoke night at a local dive bar. The night was a terrific one. They even got me to sing, something I imagine was an ordeal for all concerned. Nevertheless, I was invited to go again the next Friday and told them I would. I even considered bringing Lexi. Her singing voice would make up for mine and everyone would love her.

It was, if not a new beginning, then at least the first real attempt at one. Before I found the blanket, I couldn't remember the last time I'd laughed without forcing it, or enjoyed anything without letting the guilt crucify me afterward.

Loneliness awaited me at home, but it was offset greatly by the promise of what my life now held: new friends, a social life, and a renewed relationship with my wife. So, when I sat down before my sitcoms, beer in hand, it was not so much a desperate escape as a pleasant and enjoyable one.

To cap it all, I got a rather unexpected phone call the following Tuesday afternoon. It was from Lexi's father, Joe, a man whose apparent coolness toward me could be traced back to that one Christmas Eve when I admitted while sitting with him before a OSU V Clemson game that I'd never much cared for sports. To a diehard Buckeye and the kind of man's man the world just doesn't seem to produce anymore, that was akin to confessing that I liked to burn flags and speak Russian in my spare time. Okay, maybe not *that* dramatic, but whatever my ill-advised admission instilled in him, he'd never been very warm to me after that, his gaze somewhat withering, his smiles plastic when aimed in my direction. Lex had always assured me I was imagining it, but I knew better. It's easy to tell when you're the least liked person in the room. As far as I could recall, I'd never received a phone call from Joe that hadn't been meant for Lexi, so when I saw his name on my cell screen, I was filled with sudden dread. It couldn't mean anything good. Maybe he was calling to tell me to back off his daughter, that it was only going to cause her more hurt, or maybe to inform me of his true feelings once and for all.

You couldn't even keep my granddaughter alive, you piece of shit. Why on earth do you think I'd trust you to keep my Lexi safe?

Mouth dry, I jabbed the button to accept the call. "Hello?"

"Steve?" *Steve?*

"Yeah, hey Joe. Is everything okay?"

"Huh? Oh yes, fine, fine. Everything's just fine."

When he didn't say anything, I filled the silence. "What can I do for you?"

"Huh?"

It was like I'd wandered in on his conversation with himself.

"Oh, I just wanted to call. To call you. It was Marcy's idea, really. I thought she might call you. I got back from work and she said she hadn't...yet...so she said I might as well just go ahead and...you know...do it, so..."

I put a hand to my mouth to stifle the laughter. Already this was likely to go down in history as the most awkward conversation I'd ever had, and that included our fateful Christmas exchange, which had concluded with him looking at me in confusion and saying, "If a man doesn't like football, I just don't know what he *can* like."

I decided to be merciful. "Well, I'm happy to hear from you, Joe. It's been a while."

"It has, yes. It has. Awful business what happened. Was so very sorry to hear it. Poor little thing. Terrible loss."

Little thing. The enormity of her passing has always rendered such descriptions redundant.

"Did you want to speak to me about something, Joe?"

"What? Oh, yes. I, that is to say we, Marcy and I, and Lexi, of course, wanted to ask if you'd be at all interested in joining us for dinner tomorrow night. I think she's making lasagna. Marcy, I mean. Don't know if you like lasagna, but I think hers is pretty good. Best I've ever had, anyway."

"I'd love to. What time?"

"Huh? Uh, hey, what time?" he yelled, and I heard Marcy respond a moment before he did. "Say, eight? Does that work? Eight o' clock?"

"It does indeed."

"See you at eight, then?"

"Wouldn't miss it."

For the rest of the day I felt like my blood had been replaced by sunlight. The guilt lingered in the wings, of course, and I suspected it would be some time before any degree of happiness did not demand a fair and merciless accounting, because at the end of the day grieving people are not supposed to be happy. But damn it, I couldn't help it. And I needed it. Things were changing. A few weeks before, I'd thought I was destined to suffer alone, thought I had lost my wife in addition to my child. But now Lexi had let me back in, her family had let me back in, and I could at least allow myself a moment of celebration for how that made me feel.

Every Monday morning in class, I asked my students to draw on a piece of paper an emoji that best reflected how their weekend had gone and hold it up before their faces. Invariably, the faces were happy, sometimes, sad, which would lead to a discussion about what had gone wrong—assuming the child wanted to discuss it, of course—and we would try to dissolve the negativity through a class discussion. Positive reinforcement to counter negative experience, because ultimately, nobody wants to face the bad things alone.

It was my hope now, that I would no longer have to.

* * *

That night, as I lay in bed, drifting off to sleep, my cell phone hummed. To my delight, the text was from Lexi. It read: "Harder to sleep alone now that I've been reminded what it's like when I don't have to :)"

Beneath the words was an overhead selfie of her lying in bed, the sheets and her bra pulled down to reveal her breasts. Her nipples were hard. The smile on her face was coquettish, seductive, and full of promise, eyes glimmering in the light from her bedside lamp.

I responded: "I'll be there in five minutes. With or without pants."

"My parents would love that."

"Do I at least get to stay over tomorrow night?"

"I'm sure you could if you wanted to. Just don't talk football with Dad. :)"

"Believe me, I've learned my lesson."

"And we'd have to be quiet. They go to bed early."

"*Me* be quiet? You're the one with the volume control issues."

"Only when you do good."

"Well, I intend to, so I may have to gag you."

"Ooh, kinky."

"I know, right? Short leap from there to whips and chains."

She laughed at that. My favorite sound in the world.

"So, Mom's excited to have you over."

"Really?"

"Yeah. She always liked you. Even after we lost Robin, and I came to hide away here, she asked about you a lot. She worried."

This was news to me, and while I couldn't speak to the veracity of my wife's words—it was entirely likely she was just laying the groundwork for the next night's get-together—I appreciated hearing it.

"Well, I've always liked her too."

"I'm looking forward to tomorrow night, to things feeling normal, like before. Is that wrong?"

"Hell no, it's not wrong. You deserve this. We both do. And your family does too."

"Good. Well, I should get some sleep. I've got a busy day ahead of me tomorrow."

"Send me another picture before you go."

"Horndog."

"You know it."

For a few moments, the phone was silent, then a picture of her popped up on the screen. It was a close-up of her mouth, those wonderful lips parted enticingly, the nail of her forefinger pressed against the lower one.

It was followed by one last text: "See you tomorrow night, lover. Be sure to bring your appetite."

* * *

That night, I had a terrible dream. I was lying on the floor in a house I didn't know, a dirty house, little more than a cabin, with small windows occluded by yellow dirt and clotted with old cobwebs, their architects long dead. The ceiling was oppressively low and crisscrossed by huge timber beams still wearing their bark. The floor, what little I could see of it, was fashioned from similar material. Crowding the area around me were dozens upon dozens of antique dolls, all of them seated around me like an audience before a stage. Some were porcelain; some were straw, others were made of what appeared to be clay. Why they might be positioned as if to give me their attention was a mystery, however, because their heads were turned away from me, toward the opposite end of the room, to the woman seated at the rickety kitchen table.

The light was dim in the room, and what little there was came from no discernible source, so I only had the faintest impression of the woman. She looked like a clothes horse made of bones, the material hanging from her skeletal frame as dirty as the room in which she sat. Her dark matted hair hung in clumps over her face and she nodded jerkily along to the arrhythmic tapping of her long yellow nails on the table top.

As I lay there, stricken, I began to feel that tapping radiating up through the floorboards into my chest, rapping at my heart, forcing my teeth to clack together, invoking dread in me that I was in some lethal, alien place I would never escape even by waking. I tried to move and found that the sleeves of my shirt, which were fashioned from the same rotten material the woman and some of the dolls wore, had been nailed to the floor with rusty ingots. The cuffs of my threadbare pants, the same. My feet were streaked with dirt, and were most definitely not mine. The toenails were curled and yellow and spotted with something dark. I opened my mouth to scream and choked instead as a thick black thread spun out and upward from the back of my throat before snapping free to vanish up into the darkness of the rafters. There was no time to try to make out where it had gone, because now there came a leathery creaking sound, like someone twisting a belt in their hands.

I turned my head in time to see all the dolls do the same.

All of them looked at me in unison as the woman rose up, blocking the light from the room.

Fingers protruded from their eyesockets, too small to belong to adults.

Too pink and spongy to be fake.

Their mouths gaped hungrily.

The woman reached her full height and I strained to follow her progress. She was tall, impossibly tall now, and had to bend to avoid colliding with the rafters. Her arms, with those awful spindly fingers, seemed to grow toward me like a time-lapse video of kudzu vines. Her belly began to swell outward until she resembled some massive sea creature fished dead and bloated from the tide. I smelled dirt and blood and sour milk, glimpsed purplish skin sloughing off the woman's wrists to spatter on the floor and thought the dolls might have scurried to retrieve it. All I knew for sure was that they had moved as one toward the area of the floor where the blood was thickest.

The room began to shudder and quake. Dust rained down from the rafters as they cracked and splintered. The woman continued to grow, the dolls continued to move. And feed. The stench thickened and I knew she was going to reach me soon, struggled against the nails pinning me to the rotten floor. The light began to bleed out of the room, eclipsed by this enormous creature as it continued to swell, swell, swell, bigger, and bigger, and bigger, until she seemed to fill my vision without ever having left the other side of the room.

And then her face was hanging over me and I screamed in absolute mind-shearing horror at the sight of what had been hiding beneath that caul of hair, until the dolls found my mouth and begin to climb inside, their tiny hands warm against my lips, my tongue…

* * *

When I woke with a cry, I thought the nightmare had followed me, that the woman had filled the room, blocking the sunlight. Thought I glimpsed her shrinking back into the shadows beyond the foot of the bed, thought the dolls might have scurried underneath it, just waiting for me to go back to sleep. After a panicked moment, I realized it was still night, still dark, and that my phone was ringing. No, not ringing. Tapping. I'd fallen asleep and had knocked it off the bed and now it was vibrating against the hardwood floor, making the same sound I had ascribed to the witch (for surely that's what she'd been.) Maybe not the same sound, but close enough to fuel a nightmare if the sleeper had an overactive imagination, something of which I have frequently been accused.

I waited for my heartbeat to regulate and my breathing to follow, then leaned over and scooped the cell phone off the floor. It was Lexi, and she was video-calling me at three a.m.

Disorientated and confused—why would she be calling me at such an hour?—I reached over, turned on the bedside lamp and tapped the green button to accept the call.

It took a moment for my eyes to adjust to the light. Even longer to adjust to what was on my screen as it bloomed to life on the display.

At first, I thought I was looking at Lexi tossing in her sleep, which would have begged the question of how she'd made the call, unless it was by accident. But then the screen tilted back and I was able to see her head. Her face. Her mouth.

And I screamed so loudly in horror it roused the neighbors from their beds and brought them hammering at my door. I ignored them, fell sideways off the bed and slammed my head against the floor. In my terror, I didn't know what I was supposed to do. Hang up? Or call someone? Sense permeated the panic and I killed the call, then immediately dialed her parents. They didn't answer and with each beep of that accursed busy signal, I punched the floor so hard my knuckles split and bled. Maybe they were already calling the police. *Please, God...*

Then I was up and running, pausing only to throw on a pair of pants, no shirt, no socks and shoes, and yanked open the front door, pushing past my startled neighbors, Harriet Dean and her husband Tony. "Call the police," I yelled at them, "Call them and send them to 81....*fuck*, no, *88* Market House Lane in Grandview. The Jacobsons." I tripped, stumbled, crawled to my car, fell into the driver seat and gunned the engine, mowing down my trashcans in my haste to get to where I desperately needed to be, all the while screaming at the reality that I was never going to make it.

Because I knew, knew, *knew* in my heart and in my head, in everything that mattered and would never matter to me again, that Lexi would be dead by the time I reached her.

4

THE REST OF THAT EARLY MORNING is a dream, the events seen through a flickering confusion of red and blue lights. As I wandered like a broken puppet from my car to Lexi's parents' house, what little rational thought remained in my beleaguered skull told me that this was just an extension of that monstrous nightmare from before, that nothing so cruel could happen to a person twice. It was countered by the insidious notion that if it had happened, it was certainly no coincidence. Which of course, I knew. I'd seen the truth on my cellphone screen. I just hadn't been able to fully process it yet.

It took me twenty-five minutes to reach the house, and when I arrived, my feet padded by the carpet of dead wet leaves from the walnut trees overhanging the Jacobson's drive, the police and EMTs were already there. The sun had not yet risen, but the world was lit by the silent flashing lights of the emergency vehicles, which turned the night to hellish day and sent odd shadows racing across the façade of the two-story Colonial and into the surrounding flora.

I walked as if submerged in the deep, my vision pulsing in time with my heart, my hair standing on end, mouth dry. This wasn't real. Couldn't be.

And yet it was.

A young police officer who looked perfectly suited for babysitting, and little else, broke away from a discussion with his female partner and approached me, hand held up at chest level. "Sorry sir, you can't go—"

"She's my wife," I said, my voice small and alien to my ears. His face lost none of its practiced impassivity, but he lowered his hand.

"Sir, I'm sorry to tell you there's been an—" He paused to consider his words. "—incident involving your wife. I'm afraid she's dead, sir."

You were going to say accident, I thought. *But that's not quite right and you know it. Everyone here knows it...*

Dazed, I looked past him to the front door where the Jacobsons were watching a stretcher bearing a body beneath a sheet being guided down their stoop, and felt my gorge rise. Lexi's parents were like gray, melting statues, worn down to nothing by the horror of all they'd lived to see, the horror we shared.

...because slipping in the bathtub is an accident...

Lexi's mother was screaming. Her husband was doing his best to support her weight against him, but his knees looked in danger of giving out at any moment. I looked from them to the gurney, to the bland simplicity of a shape that had held such import in my life, and the strength left me.

...falling down the stairs is an accident...

I only barely registered the pain of my knees driving those dead leaves down into the gravel as I fell and vomited all over the officer's shoes.

...but, in any sane, reasonable world, choking to death on your dead child's blanket is not.

* * *

The police helped me to a cruiser, where I sat in the back with the door open and my head bowed, not looking at that stretcher being loaded into the back of an ambulance, not looking at Lexi's parents for fear I would only see the same demand for answers I had seen the day we buried my daughter. *Why did this happen, Steve? Why did she die? How could this happen?* And most damning and haunting of all: *Why didn't you protect her?* I hated them in that moment as I sat awash in the pulse of the emergency lights, a string of bile dangling from my lips like a silver thread until it detached and disappeared into the darkness between my feet. I hated the look

I imagined on their faces without even knowing for sure it was there. But even if it wasn't, it would come. Over the coming days and weeks, it would come, and it would persist. Once the shock subsided, they would hate me for this just as I hated them for having every reason in the world to feel that way. Grief is so much easier when there's someone to blame. And what defense did I have? Robin *would* still be alive if I hadn't left that blanket in the crib with her. And Lexi *would* still be alive if she hadn't run away to hide from our daughter's loss, and worse, if I hadn't found that fucking blanket.

Blanky. Such an innocuous name for something that had now cemented itself as the locus of my grief and horror and rage.

Later, as the ambulance drove quietly away, the female officer I had seen earlier joined me in the backseat of the cruiser and offered me the standard platitudes. It reminded me of Lexi's rage against condolences and those who casually and meaninglessly deploy them. It's the most natural thing in the world, and the most useless, so I cut off the officer's sympathy with a declaration I hoped might be of more use.

"I saw her."

"Sir?"

"She called me. Facetimed me."

"Your wife?"

"Yes."

She took out a notepad and began to scribble. "When was this?"

"Three a.m."

"What did she say?"

"Nothing."

"She didn't say anything?"

I shook my head, my voice completely devoid of emotion. "She was too busy choking to death."

Pen poised above the pad, the officer looked at me squarely. Perhaps there was suspicion there, who knows? It hardly mattered. If some confluence of events pointed at me as a person of interest, I'd gladly let them take me in, and, if they made a case, throw me in jail. What else was there left for me in the world out here but misery?

"You saw her choking?"

"Yes."

"On the blanket?" *And it was moving like a living thing.*

"Yes."

"Was there anyone else in the room with her?"

"I don't know. I don't think so."

"Did it look like she might be doing it to herself. On purpose?"

"I don't know. Maybe." *No.*

"And what did you do?"

"I tried to call the house."

"Yes, we did too. Looks like the Jacobsons leave their house phone off the hook when they go to bed."

"I know. I forgot that. So, I told my neighbors to call you guys and then I drove over here."

"You stopped to ask the neighbors for help?" Definitely the faintest trace of suspicion now.

"Yes."

"You didn't think to do it yourself?"

"I was panicked, and they were there. At my door."

"At three a.m.?"

"Yes. They heard me screaming, I guess."

She stared at me for a few moments without saying anything. Probing me, perhaps, for the telltale signs of a man pantomiming the emotions expected of him upon learning his wife has died. Looking for the tell, the slipping of the mask, the shark beneath the surface. And for all I knew, I probably looked guilty as hell because I don't believe I was displaying any emotion at all. I was numb.

So I asked her. "Do you think I had something to do with this?"

She shook her head. "Some people think it strengthens the spiritual connection to exit their lives the same way as those they've lost. I am truly sorry to hear about your daughter, by the way."

By the way. My daughter, the afterthought.

"But, that'll do for now. If I have any further questions, we have your address." She pocketed the notepad and slid out of the car. "I'll get someone to take you home. I think the best thing you can do is get some rest. The next few days will be hard. And again, I'm sorry for your loss, Mr. Brannigan. Truly, I am."

The words, like acid, bubbled up my throat and were out of my mouth before I knew they were coming. "And what the fuck would you know about loss? You're just the uniform who tells people about their own. You're a fucking accountant for other people's misery."

Clearly jolted by my outburst, she put a hand on the roof of the cruiser and leaned in to look at me, her face obscured by the dark. "My father shot himself when I was in grade school, so, I know plenty. Everybody has to endure it eventually. Death is part of life, and I sympathize that you've seen so much of it lately. Now go home, Mr. Brannigan."

* * *

They drove me home and the guilt chased me like a living thing, hiding in every shadowed pocket between the houses and hedges, hunkering just outside the sodium pools of light from the streetlamps, and sneering at me from the wedges of dark beneath the silent cars parked at the side of the road. Somehow, I managed to croak a thank you to the officers and walked like a zombie up the short path to the front door of my house. I didn't want to go inside and instead stood with my key in the lock for what felt like forever, until the sky was turning pink and the shadows were forced to retreat. Only then, with nowhere else to go, did I concede defeat and admit myself once more into the sepulcher of disaster where this nightmare had begun.

Inside, I stood in my living room staring down at the sofa where Lexi had sat stroking Robin's blanket, where we'd reconnected after my fears that she was gone forever. And now she was. There were no tears this time though, no self-pity, no buckling agony. Only rage.

I looked from the sofa to the coffee table where in the light from the TV I could still see the hardened rings of condensation where we'd left our drinks sit overnight.

I stalked to the kitchen cabinet and filled a glass to the brim with whiskey. There was a good chance I had some Vicodin somewhere too. I'd find those later and not stop until my heart did.

If this utterly fucking warped life was going to take from me all that I loved, then why not join them?

Nobody wants to live alone in the dark, and from my vantage point, I could see no tomorrow.

* * *

In the morning, there were twelve messages on my phone, seven of them from Lexi's parents' number, one from the Columbus Police Department, another from Principal Lewis. I deleted them all. Crawling out of bed in a fog of confusion and self-loathing, I was not in the mood to be berated or made to feel like a suspect, or worse, a victim. I had more pressing concerns, like trying to put one foot in front of the other without vomiting my intestines all over the floor.

The light through the partially open blinds was, like me, feeble and gray. I felt like my bones had been replaced by marbles, which rattled chaotically around every time I grew ambitious and tried to speed up my progress. I could not stop clenching my teeth, which, considering the deep ache in my jaw, seemed to have been a condition that had started in my sleep.

But I couldn't think of sleep, or the horrific images—
the woman
the dolls
the fingers and blood
—that had populated it again, or it might have sent me screaming out of the house, an act that already seemed like an eventuality considering all that had happened in such a short space of time.

A reliance on mundane preprogramming led me to the breakfast nook, where I poured myself a bowl of Frosted Flakes, added milk, and sat down on the stool munching and staring at the backyard. It looked as it always had, albeit leached of color by the monochrome day.

The grass needed mowing. I'd been too preoccupied, too—dare I say it—enlivened by hope—to bother with it.

The door in the high wooden fence was squeaking in its frame despite being latched, as it had done over the past few months. The hinges needed oiling.

There was a tree in the center of the yard which provided merciful shade in the cruel heat of Ohio summers. But summer was long gone now and the tree had shed its leaves. They lay like a multicolored rug at its feet.

I stopped chewing and dropped the spoon into the bowl, splashing milk on my chest.

A woman sat in the shade of that walnut tree now, her back to the trunk, her knees drawn up, head lowered in the protective cradle of her arms, perhaps to avoid the discomfort of her skull meeting the gnarled lower branches, though they were higher than I could reach even on tiptoe. She wore a white nightdress, much as the woman from my dream had done. It was threadbare, marred by stains of indeterminate origin. The flesh of her arms was exposed, the skin mottled blue-gray.

Slowly I rose, the chair tipping over and startling me as it crashed to the floor.

I swallowed, heard my throat click, my lips instantly dry.

I had seen this woman in my sleep, assumed both she and the gruesome scene in which she had played the starring role had been nothing more than the mad product of stress and hope and grief and despair, a subconscious mural meant to make sense to no one. A strange one-act play in the theater of dreams.

But now she was here.

Reason suggested I pull the blinds shut over the screen door and seek help, whether that help came in the form of more alcohol, more sleep, or fleeing the scene, mattered little. Anything other than what I already knew I was going to do. Maybe because I knew if she wanted to come for me, the door wouldn't stop her. Walls wouldn't stop her. If she could saunter into my subconscious unobstructed, anything I tried to do would only be delaying the inevitable.

Trembling, I grabbed the metal handle of the rain-speckled glass door.

The woman raised her head, damp hair still hanging in her face, and as she cocked it slightly in my direction, I was blinded by a flash of lightning, a dazzling blue pulse that forced my hand up to cover my eyes.

When I lowered them a few seconds later, vision still filled with dancing orbs and dervishing sparks, she was standing before the half-open door, allowing me to see through the shock and the confusion, that it was not the woman from my dream after all, but my wife, Lexi, albeit it not an interpretation of her I would ever have wished to see.

I screamed and recoiled, my ankles colliding with the fallen stool to send me tumbling backward, my spine meeting the hard wooden seat in just the right way to send radial explosions of pain through my body. But I barely felt it as I scrabbled away and my wife, this version of her so tall she had to stoop, stepped into the room.

She was soaking wet from the rain, her bare feet leaving ragged muddy prints on the tile.

Her skin was gray. Her eyes were gone. From the sockets, infant fingers waggled in a parody of farewell. And though she spoke, her words were lost to me, because Blanky, the blanket she'd choked to death on, was still lodged in her throat, one frayed end of it flapping in the breeze like an obscenely swollen and distended tongue. And on that tongue, I saw one of the faded rabbits, its eyes burning coals, skin tattooed with faintly glowing blue symbols, as she lowered her face down toward where I lay helpless on the floor. Her hair, now blonde and not black at all, tickled my cheek as I raised my arms and shrieked to ward off what must, what could only be a product of incumbent madness. She could not be here. This was not real. I must be dreaming.

But then those infant fingers poking from my wife's empty eyesockets touched my skin, Blanky found my mouth, the cotton wet against my lips, and I knew none of those realities were the active one.

My wife was dead.

My wife was here.

She smiled at me and her face became something else, the same face from the dream, a face that will forever evade my ability to properly describe it without utterly breaking down, because it was no face at all, just a hollow filled with darkness, though if I dared stare into that cranial abyss for a second too long, I could almost see something moving in there. Lights or stars. Or maybe that was still a product of the retinal distress caused by the lightning.

Whatever it was, it infected me, rendered my whole body numb.

I might have smiled, might even have laughed. Certainly, I wept.

It felt like a mercy to allow it to take me.

* * *

There is no sadness where she lives. There is nothing. Everything here in this dirty little house in the middle of the woods is simple, forgotten, but useful. She exists not to cause pain, at least not as man thinks of pain, but freedom from the tethers of an ugly world she only vaguely understands. She is unique and terrible and content, for the most part, to be left to her own devices. But a woman who came from another place cannot be allowed to live here without her origin and nature being challenged at every turn. In the villages where The Others live, she is a thing to be feared, a Thing of Whispers. To them, she is The Other, which on some level she understands.

For decades, they have attempted to draw her out, sent expeditions of their bravest and most violent men to challenge her. She does not need to see or speak to them to know they have little interest in peace or understanding. She can feel their intent, their fear, their bloodlust, as soon as they rise in the morning seventy miles south of where she sits whispering to the dolls.

She feels no sadness, no remorse, no rueful wishes that things could be different.

She is not a being that can feel anything at all.

To the crusaders who seek out her destruction, she is Evil. It is a word they utter often in their taverns over tankards of bitter ale, their faces drawn by fear. Evil is the word that rises from the murk of their incomprehension. They have branded her with it.

Evil.

And Witch.

She ponders the irony of trying to cast in unflattering light, a creature that knows only the dark.

And though their language is mostly alien to her, she is able to draw their meaning from the images in their minds when they use such words. She knows also that she is none of these things, but to attempt to make them understand this, even if she sought to plant the truth in their heads, even if she cared enough to try, would be a waste of her time, and would undoubtedly drive them mad. They should not persist in trying to define her. Such pursuits are foolhardy and will end in their destruction, something of which they are intimately aware, and yet they persist in trying to end her.

The truth is that she is nothing at all, hardly a presence, certainly not a being. She is little more than a tool of uncaring and uncivilized gods and thus they would do well to avoid her.

Yet still they come, men who see her only as something to be punished. Absent this fear, she might have been invisible to them. Still, she senses their faces at the window, feels the heat from the torches in their hands. Long before she permits those blood-filled wastrels entry, they have already been undone by their own fear, their own uncertainty in the face of The One True Nothing.

Their sacrifice upon her altar is not quick, but it is necessary, for although she can subsist on the bad dreams of others and autumn breezes alone, the children need to feed.

5

THE SUN CAME OUT; THE SUN WENT DOWN. The phone rang endlessly until I smashed it against the wall. I ignored the people knocking at the door. The Deans, I assumed. Nice people who had forever been a little too nosy, a little too eager to invite themselves into our lives. I recalled Lexi being uncomfortable at just how attentive they were to the mound of her pregnant belly, like they were auditioning for a remake of *Rosemary's Baby*. How Harriet had cooed and put her face close to Lexi's stomach and spoke as if my wife's body was a tin can phone connected to the baby inside. And all the while, her husband Tony stood much too close to me, nodding knowingly, as if pregnancy was some great conspiracy we had let him in on. The winks, the soft punches to the shoulder, like *Gee whiz, kid, ain't this something special?*, which, coming from a man who had never spawned children of his own, seemed forced and out of place.

Busybodies.

Eventually the knocking became more forceful. They must have called the police with stories of screams and falling furniture. The thin walls between our houses had probably been a prime source of entertainment for them over the years, from arguments and laughter, to loud sex and the prematurely silenced wailing of the resultant child. I imagine them sitting with their matching armchairs pressed against the walls, their heads back, eyes hooded, mouths turned up in dazed, creepy smiles like emotional vampires as they imagined what we might be doing next door. Lately, I suspected I had turned their vicarious auditory voyeurism to outright alarm.

I lay on the floor before the open screen door, relishing the chill from the wind and the rain as it blew in on me like sea-spray. My wife, or the thing that had worn her costume, was gone and I was not dead. I felt no relief from this realization as the pounding on the door worked in synch with the beating of my heart.

I believed she had been here. I could still taste damp cotton in my mouth and remembered the whispery caress of tiny fingers against my cheeks. Recalled the smell of sour milk. She had come here and she had taken me away for a spell, yanked me, or maybe just my mind, through the hollow where her face should have been into…someplace else. The place from my feverish dreams. A place I now believed to be real.

Unbidden, I thought of my parents. Good people who came from nothing and yet found a way to pay for my education, perhaps in the hope that I would make them prouder than they'd ever been able to make themselves. I remember my father, a carpenter, laboring away over a length of pine he had propped up between sawhorses. I recall the smile when he saw me sitting atop a cabinet in his workshop, watching him intently, and the wistfulness he always seemed to carry in his eyes. "You know," he told me once, "I tell people I'm a man of the world. And I think that's true." Then his smile had faded a little with what could have been the first sign of the confusion that would ultimately cloud his mind and kill him at the ripe old age of sixty-four. "I'm just not always sure which one."

My mother was also sometimes given to such cryptic ponderings and hers alarmed me no less than my father's. I'm not even sure I always understood what they were telling me, or even if they understood it themselves, but the sadness with which their words were delivered was never lost on me. For reasons that remain a mystery, they always seemed mournful. On my worst days, I tell myself my entry into their lives did not so much fill a vacuum as create one. They were good people, but never completely there. They were like portraits of themselves.

"You're lucky to have us," my mother always said, with what I took at the time to be humor, but can't recall the smile. "I never knew my parents, and they didn't know me." When once, I broached this claim with her parents, my grandparents, they seemed genuinely baffled by her words, and assured me I had misheard them. But I know I didn't, and entered into my adolescence convinced I had been raised by ghosts.

The muted squawk and hiss of a police radio broke through my reverie. Flares of pain jolted my back, made me wince as I struggled to get to my feet, one hand braced on the counter to keep from falling.

The place I had seen...the ill-lighted cabin, the room, the woman, and the dolls. It was there. I had felt her, the slight bristling of the long coarse hairs on the nape of her neck at the sense that people were yet again, indomitably, encroaching on her domain. What I didn't yet know was what it all meant, but I was damn sure now that it meant *something*, perhaps the key to everything that had happened thus far. And that awareness left me with two possibilities, neither one of which I found unappealing:

If I could find out what and where that woman's sanctuary was, perhaps I could stay there forever in a hell that would welcome me for all that I had done. Or all that I hadn't. A fitting end for my failure as both parent and husband. That it might be little more than the visualization of my own madness didn't alter what it would represent should I reach it.

Or I could destroy it, and Blanky, and at least die knowing I had saved someone else from the nightmare that had consumed my life.

But through it all, no matter which way the pendulum swung, I was still left with one desperate need: to know why. Why had this happened to me? What kind of ungodly force could so callously take away my family with nary a pause for breath between executions? What had I really done to deserve this?

"Mr. Brannigan?" A stern voice through the front door. Could they just come in unannounced? Would my failure to respond be adequate cause for them to barge their way in? Too much TV told me they probably could, and I knew I could not be there when that happened.

I rushed to the closet, grabbed my overcoat with its too-tight buttons, and shrugged it on. I stepped into my trainers and exited out the screen door, sliding it slowly shut behind me, cutting off the concerned officer's final summons.

I had no desire to grant an audience to people who thought worse of me than I did myself. So instead I went to the only safe place left that would have me.

* * *

I stayed at the bar until the choice was removed and the drinks stopped coming. The night is a blur after that, though I can vaguely recall heading to the square where the Columbus Market vendors gather on Sundays, where Mr. Baby Close had sold Lexi the blanket that murdered her and our child. It was empty of course but for a three-legged dog engaged in warfare with a greasy Wendy's bag, and a breeze that carried the faint smell of smoke. I took a bench and mulled incoherently over my options until I became convinced that there was something watching me from the darkness beyond the ranks of streetlights.

Somehow, I found my way home, where, mercifully there was nobody at the door, and tried to find solace in an episode of *Barney Miller* but it was too hard to focus on his tough yet congenial face, and eventually, I passed out.

In the dream, she was telling them a story...

The next day, Lexi's parents tried calling again. I quite simply didn't know what to say to them, so I didn't pick up. I had already run this gauntlet after Robin's death, and I didn't know how to do it anymore. And for them, this was worse. Robin had been our child; Lexi was theirs. I knew all too well the horror of that unique and soul-destroying loss.

And of course, I knew, no matter how unfair, that they would blame me. Every day I refused to take their calls only made it worse.

But I couldn't avoid them at the funeral, not unless I didn't attend, and that was never going to be an option. Despite all the horrors associated with what had happened and the things that had come to find me in the wake of them, I loved Lexi and would never have been able to forgive myself if I didn't say goodbye.

* * *

Outside of those first few times in the beginning, I had actively avoided coming to see Robin's grave. It was, as she had been in her all too brief life, so small and so new that the sight of her name chiseled into cold uncaring stone was enough to drain my will to go on each and every time I was faced with it. So I started making excuses not to visit, a decision that guts me now.

On the day of the funeral, that's where I found Lexi's parents, not before the grave of their daughter, with the coffin propped above it, but at Robin's. I stood behind them, relishing those few moments in which I did not register to them. I did not look at my child's grave. Instead I focused on my one-time parents-in-law. Joe had his arm around Marcy's shoulders, which were spasming as she wept against him. I looked from them to the people slowly making their way across the cemetery to my wife's grave, and wondered how any of this had happened. It felt surreal in the worst way, like waking up to find yourself in a room

full of dolls with babyfingers for eyes

with no doors and no idea how you got there or how to get out. Self-preservation is an amazing thing. It can make fighters of the fallen and summon determination from the dust, but it can't last forever, especially in the face of overwhelming odds. When you're being beaten, sometimes it's best just to stop struggling and embrace the end. Sometimes you can even convince yourself you deserve it.

"Steve?"

I flinched and looked at Joe. His face was the color of a dust cloth, his eyes sunken in their sockets. If there was a reprimand there, I didn't see it. At his summons, Marcy turned to look at me and she looked even worse. I thought of faded paintings in dusty attics. Behind them, the bare branches of the sycamore trees clacked together like bones. Red and yellow leaves tussled across grass that was one rain shy of needing a haircut.

I opened my mouth to say something and only the breeze came out. My throat tightened and as I willed myself to speak, I saw their faces melt like wax and then they were upon me, all sobs and fumbling arms and clambering hands. At first I stiffened, possessed of the crazy notion that maybe they were attacking me, trying to suffocate me or squeeze me to death, but at Marcy's whisper in my ear—"I'm so, so, *sorry*, Steven"—I finally broke down and let loose the torrent of pain that had held me in its thrall for what seemed like years.

"We tried to call you," Marcy said, with Joe content to nod along in sympathetic agreement. His eyes were red and swollen now, his lower lip quivering, which I guess is about as much emotion as a man's man will allow himself. I wouldn't know. I hate football, remember?

"I know," I told them. Marcy's eyes seemed to be reaching deep inside mine, looking for the fragments of my heart so that she could assist me in putting them back together. "I'm sorry. I was...I needed some time."

"She loved you," Marcy said, her words shaky as more tears pricked her eyes. "My God, she loved you so much."

I nodded, gave her the best smile I could muster, which was no smile at all, and put a hand on her shoulder.

"You're family," she said. "We want you to know that. Don't we, Joe?"

"Yes," he said, and though he looked mildly uncomfortable, I took him at his word. "Of course. Our home is your home. Stop by anytime." He could have been speaking to an old friend after a backyard barbecue, but I appreciated the gesture.

Later, as we stood shoulder to shoulder, me and my borrowed family of broken people, we watched in silence with a crowd of strangers as the morose priest read words that meant nothing to me and they lowered down into the earth the only woman who did. The device used to facilitate the coffin's descent shuddered and whined as if it too opposed the senselessness of it all. Around us the leaves scratched and the breeze hissed through the grass. The overcast sky mumbled of thunder.

I expected to be assailed by memories of my life with Lexi as they lowered the coffin, images of her face, her eyes, her smile, auditory recollections of the funniest and sweetest things she'd said to me since that rainy night I met her outside of a Costco and offered her the shelter of my umbrella. But I saw none of these things.

And when, after the roses had been thrown into the hole in the earth, Marcy leaned over to me and whispered, "We put Robin's blanket in there with her," I could only back away and stare at her in abject horror until those strangers were coming to my aid and I was fighting them off and then running, running, running back toward the car and away from this garden of death and madness. I had to, because the only other course of action, the first to present itself as the rational course of action, was to jump down into the grave, tear open the coffin, and rip that blanket out of there.

I didn't want that fucking malevolent thing anywhere near my wife's body.

It was the reason she was dead in the first place.

Worse, it had taken me seeing Lexi's grave and hearing her mother's words to realize why we hadn't seen that blanket in the weeks after Robin's death. We'd mistakenly assumed the paramedics had used it to cover our infant's body when they took it away. But they hadn't. In all the chaos of that night, it had remained behind in her crib until we brought it to the funeral home and tucked it into her coffin a few days later.

We should never have seen Blanky again.

Because we buried her with it.

And as I drove home screaming at the windshield and the world beyond it, all I could picture was that foul dirty blanket in Lexi's coffin, crawling slowly and inexorably toward my dead wife's mouth.

* * *

I lost track of my days and nights, spent many of them seated beneath the tree where I saw, or thought I saw, the woman from the dream who became my wife and took me away to that other place. And every time I thought of how calmly and casually I accepted those events, the needle on the insanity meter began to inch a little closer into the red.

The progression of events was thus:

Robin died, suffocated in her crib by an old blanket, and we, addled by sentiment, had buried her with it.

And it had come back. Neither of us could or would recall putting Blanky in the coffin because we didn't want to. It was an emotional connection to our lost little girl, no matter how it had appeared, and we were as unwilling to question that as we were to let go of it.

Then Lexi died, choked to death on the same blanket.

And there was only one person who could tell me why.

6

I UNDERSTAND OF COURSE," Principal Lewis said. "You'll be missed a great deal. By the staff, but mostly by your students."

A rotund and cheerful man, Lewis regarded me as one might a drug addicted relative, with a caution borne of affection. His brows were furrowed slightly, his smile strained.

"We were of course, all of us, devastated to hear of your loss."

Same thing he'd said to me after Robin's death. A well-practiced line, but by then, almost two weeks after Lexi's funeral, I'd decided to let go of my derision for sympathy. If the worst thing you can say about somebody is that they tried to make you feel better when you clearly needed it, well then, who's the real asshole in that equation?

"Thanks, Bob."

He pursed his enormous lips and clasped his fingers together atop his desk. A single tuft of red hair rose from the middle of his otherwise bald skull like a flame. It was the reason the kids had nicknamed him Principal Tin-Tin.

"Would you consider an extended hiatus instead of quitting us altogether? In light of your circumstances, I have no doubt the board would understand. Take some time, take a vacation somewhere nice. Clear your head, maybe, and come back to us."

A thousand different responses came to me as I sat looking up at the anti-bullying posters on the wall behind him, none of them charitable. *Clear your head of what, exactly?* I wanted to scream at him. *The memories of my dead family?* But he didn't deserve that. His heart was now, as it had always been, in the right place. He was a good guy with bad taste in suits and a preposterous hairdo, but that didn't make him an enemy, no matter how painful his choice of words.

"I've considered it," I lied, because I hadn't considered much of anything good since the funeral. "But I think I'd only keep dragging it out and putting you in a bad situation. Better to just accept the end of the chapter and move on. It's what's fair to everybody."

And besides, by this time next week, I'll either be in jail or dead.

"I was young when I lost my father," he said, looking past me to the bloomless azalea bush outside the window of his office. "Cancer. It's tough when we lose the people closest to us. Not sure I've ever gotten over it. You have to, though, right? You just have to, or nothing makes sense anymore."

If it was a pep talk, it was a shitty one, and my expression must have conveyed that, because he focused, cleared his throat and stood with a sheepish smile, a hand extended over the desk. "I always liked you, Steve, and I hate what you've gone...what you're going through."

What I was going through was evident in how I looked. I hadn't shaved or changed my clothes in days, my eyes were bloodshot, and I was trembling uncontrollably. Meth addicts suffering through withdrawal have more composure. After glimpsing myself in the mirror before leaving for the school, I'd burst out laughing at the wretch staring back at me. It was nobody I knew.

"And you'll always have a place here with us. We're family."

Resisting the grim urge to compare his words to the those best utilized in cult indoctrination, I rose and shook his hand. "Thanks, Bob."

After a moment of awkward silence in which he looked around his office as if seeing it for the first time, he brightened and said, "You'll want to say goodbye to the kids, of course."

* * *

Classes were in session, the hallway echoing with the sounds of subdued instruction and robotic response. My footsteps sounded impossibly loud on the tile as I took in the light blue rows of lockers on either side of me. Naturally, graffiti was forbidden, and yet this rule had gone largely ignored. As I neared my classroom door, I saw that someone had stuck a goggle-eyed cartoon ladybug on the door of their locker, and was not at all surprised.

There are no coincidences.

I was not sure I wanted to say goodbye to my students. I felt deep affection for each and every one of them (with the possible exception of the Martin kid, who, barring therapeutic intervention, was destined to become an asshole of the highest order), and I would miss them dearly, but I didn't want them to see me in my current state. Better they remember me at my best. I was also afraid of how they might treat what had happened to me. They were innocents, driven by curiosity about the world around them, and death was particularly fascinating to them. What might they ask me, and how on earth could I answer without falling apart?

Where are your wife and daughter now, Mr. Brannigan?

Well, Sam, they're in the ground. Cold and dead and waiting for the worms.

Not in Heaven?

I don't believe in Heaven, Alice, and you shouldn't either, because Heaven is a construct fabricated by people who can't let go of those they've lost and who wish to relegate the notion of personal responsibility to a ghost in the sky.

That's not what my Mom says.

Then she has a lot to learn, and so do you, and you will, eventually, when everything goes wrong in your life. I wish that wasn't what had to happen for you to find out that the edges of the world can cut you, but there you go...

You look sick, Mr. Brannigan. Are you going to die too?

I sure hope so, Katie.

The phantom discussion stayed my hand on the door handle, and instead I peered in through the tall wire-mesh window in the upper half of the door. The substitute teacher, Mrs. Jove, bane of a thousand students, was drawing what looked like a vintage baby carriage on the chalkboard. When I saw the two words she had written above it, in a childish font I knew wasn't hers, I licked my lips and backed away from the door, my heart trip-hammering in my chest. I wasn't scared, not quite. What I had endured over the past few months had finally inured me to such purposeless responses, but I still felt threatened on an atavistic level, sure now that no matter where I went, this thing, the woman, would follow me. The words on the chalkboard were her way of letting me know she was watching:

BABY CLOSE

I moved to the other side of the door so that the substitute teacher and the chalkboard were out of view, and looked instead at the students. Despite the need to be gone from there, from the crawling sensation of being monitored by forces I was thus far incapable of comprehending, I couldn't go without seeing the kids one last time.

Immediately, I wished I'd resisted the urge and just gone home.

The children were looking in my direction. All of them wore long-eared rabbit masks with black buttons for eyes, their mouths split into lascivious leers, rubber tongues lolling. Before I moved away from the door, crestfallen, the course of the next few days now clearer than ever, they each brought sheets of paper up from their desks to obscure their faces. It was the emoji game I had devised for them, intended to show how their weekend had gone.

But instead of sad or smiling faces, those pages now showed nothing but swirling black holes.

* * *

The lights next door were off, the Deans retired for the night, when I finally parked the car and let myself in, a bottle of Jack Daniels tucked beneath my arm.

Home, as I had always thought of it, but seldom did now, was dark and quiet.

I threw my keys on the side table and turned on the light, allowed my eyes to adjust.

And saw the thing lying on the floor of the hall.

It was stained with mud and smelling of grave dirt.

Blanky had come home too.

* * *

After donning rubber gloves from beneath the kitchen sink (I didn't want to touch it, not directly, not when I clearly recalled the jolt I had gotten when I'd picked it up from the floor of Robin's room), I picked up the blanket and spread it out flat across the coffee table in the living room. Then I turned on the overhead light, sat, glass of whiskey in hand, and for the first time ever, well and truly looked at the thing that had destroyed my life.

When Robin died, I believed it a terrible accident nobody could have foreseen or prevented. But on the night Lexi video-called me and I watched as the blanket shoved its way into her throat hard enough to break her jaw while she pulled and struggled against it, when I saw it undulate like a snake, rolling its muscles and pushing against her in a way that only something with will and the strength to accommodate it could, I knew it was acting with purpose. And if that makes me sound like an absolute lunatic, believe me, I know. But I also know what I saw. It killed my child. It killed my wife, and though it sounds like the product of an enfevered mind to claim that anything so mundane and innocuous as a child's blanket might possess nefarious intent, it also requires you to move your focus from the instrument to the owner.

Blanky was just the weapon.

And to paraphrase the old adage: weapons, alone, don't kill people.

Someone with murder in mind needs to wield them.

I traced my gloved fingers over every inch of the material, the old faded rabbits with their unkind stares watching all the while, their faces now smudged with the same mud that had been used to fill in my wife's grave. I wondered if it had ever been just a normal child's blanket or if it had been created solely to cause suffering. And why? How many people might it have killed in however long it had been around? I imagined old ladies falling asleep in front of the fire with the blanket on their laps only for their husbands to discover them in the morning, cold and blue, throats swollen and hemorrhaged eyes staring in incomprehensible horror at the ceiling. I wondered how many babies hadn't lived to see their first year because of this awful thing, how many lives it had destroyed.

And again: why?

I don't know what I expected to find, but when I reached the frayed blue linen hem of the blanket, I paused, pressed my fingertips down hard above the seams and felt resistance. There was something hard in there, sewn into the hem, and it moved beneath my touch. I put my fingers to the right and then to the left of this unyielding mass and felt more hard nubs roll beneath the material. I continued my inspection until I ended up back where I started, then went and grabbed a scissors from the drawer in the kitchen. Part of me wondered what manner of horror I might be inviting upon myself by desecrating the thing, but I had to know what I'd felt in the lining.

With no small measure of trepidation, I sat down, picked up one corner of the blanket, and, holding my breath, slid the lower blade of the scissors into the lining and jerked it upward, half-expecting it to shriek and come alive in my hands.

It did nothing of the kind.

Instead it hung limp in my grip as I poked my fingers inside the hole and worried out one of the hard objects I had felt in there. Upon realizing what I was looking at, I dropped the scissors and yanked the hem apart in my hands. The contents rained down upon the coffee table like pale white stones.

Whoever had made the blanket had filled the hem with baby teeth.

7

I CONSIDERED DESTROYING THE BLANKET, for surely it was the only sane thing to do, but after I came back from the bathroom to find the hem intact and the teeth tucked back inside it where they belonged, I realized the folly in trying. Only the scissors lying nearby indicated that I had done anything to it at all. The concern became then that I might wake in the middle of the night to find the blanket worming its way down my throat, punishment, perhaps, for daring to violate it, but even such fears couldn't counter the soporific effects of a half bottle of whiskey and soon I was asleep.

In the morning, the blanket was where I'd left it, spread out across my coffee table like the hide of a hunted animal.

I stood sipping coffee and staring at it for the longest time.

Would it scream and writhe if I burned it?

Would it stay submerged if I weighed it down with rocks and threw it into a lake?

Or would I be punished for trying?

Worse, would it summon *her?*

I took a shower, shaved myself and dressed in clothes that didn't stink of sweat and alcohol and sat at the kitchen table. I was hungry but couldn't eat, so instead I had a beer. If nothing else, it might help penetrate the noxious caul of the hangover, or at least delay it, and I waited.

The sun was out. A beautiful Sunday. The kind of day that makes one feel glad to be alive.

But not me, not now.

I checked my watch. Quarter to noon.

I drained the beer, trashed the bottle and donned the rubber gloves just long enough to stow Blanky in a plastic grocery bag. Then I tied the handles and tossed it into the trunk of my car.

Mind clearer than it had been since Robin died, I gunned the engine, backed out of the drive, (pausing only long enough to wave at Marcy next door, who was pretending not be watching me from her living room window) and headed for the Columbus Market to meet the man who had sold us the blanket.

* * *

In contrast to the last time I had been there, the market was a hive of activity. Shoppers lured from their homes by the fine weather meandered without apparent purpose through the labyrinth of booths and stalls. Merchants hollered of bargains as if this was a dock in the eighteenth century and not the civic plaza between a Chase Bank and the People's Park. Prime cuts of various meats were displayed in the shade as the vendors waved away flies. Fish of all kinds lay on trays of ice staring in openmouthed shock at nothing. Booksellers sat fanning themselves with leaflets while looking bemused at noncommittal browsers idly flipping through the titles on their tables. There were booths set up to sell pet clothing, handmade jewelry, henna tattoos, porcelain dolls (I quickly averted my gaze from *those* little fuckers), baked desserts, homemade candies, seeds and plants, shrubs and flowers, garden sheds and ornaments, birdhouses, fishing lures, and antiques. There was even a local author seated at a Formica table shilling copies of his books. His gaze showed such desperation, I couldn't meet it for long.

Away from the epicenter of vendors, a garishly painted food truck passed out gyros and kabobs to an ever-growing crowd.

The air was redolent of sweat, fried meat, cotton candy, and asphalt.

I infiltrated the throng, not even bothering to pretend I was interested in their wares, and shrugged off the more aggressive of the vendors, one of whom tried to direct me to a fortune teller, as if this was not a market after all, but a carnival. I glared at him and moved on. I didn't need to pay some overly made-up charlatan to tell me that my future was likely to be an ugly one.

After jostling my way through a crowd of people who appeared to have forsaken civility in favor of the best bargains, I thought I spotted what I was looking for, and roughly shoved aside the burly man who was obscuring my view. He turned, a red-bearded man holding an enormous gyro wrapped in foil, and glowered at me.

"The fuck's your problem?"

I just looked at him and he went away. Later he would probably sit at a bar with his friends and tell them he hoped his life never went so far down the shitter that he ended up looking like the man he'd met at the market.

He moved on through the crowd and in the brief gap he left in his wake, I saw, not four feet away, nestled snugly between a stall selling stuffed toys on one side, and wind chimes and painted lighthouses on the other, the sign that had come to mean so much: BABY CLOSE. It was painted in childish white letters on a rectangle of thin black metal. The shape of the sign and the faint suggestion of indented letters still visible between the words BABY and CLOSE indicated it might once have been a license plate. It was suspended from two small nails that had been driven into the wooden ledge that served as the booth's counter. Atop the counter were—as the sign promised—various items of clothing meant to be worn by infants: booties, tiny T-shirts with cute messages like I LOVE MOM & DAD and LATEST & GREATEST ADDITION, gowns, bodysuits, sweaters and jackets, little woolen hats and mittens.

The sight of them gave me pause.

I had come here armed with rage and vengeance, but it was impossible to look at all those tiny clothes and not remember buying them for Robin. Of course, we hadn't bought them *here*, and given what I now knew, thank Christ for that. Nevertheless, Lexi and I had spent countless hours browsing the baby stores at various malls, fawning over how cute everything was (with the occasional gasp reserved for how *expensive* it all was too). We wanted everything to be just right for Robin. We wanted her to have everything, and we broke ourselves making that happen. I can't recall ever being happier.

I heard a creak and an old man swerved into view. He'd been sitting behind the counter, head lowered, reading a newspaper, so that I hadn't seen him there at first. Now he looked up at me from his chair through thick reading glasses and smiled a smile of large yellow teeth.

"Hello, sir. Are you looking for something for the baby?"

He looked just the same as I remembered him.

His skin was tanned and well-lined, like a man who has spent much of his life laboring in the sun. Behind the glasses, one hazel-colored eye watched me with polite interest. The other was fake and watched me not at all, aimed instead at something just to the right of me. He wore a weathered old straw fedora that had passed its prime right around the time JFK took office and a pinstripe brown suit that was probably purchased on the same day. His white shirt was the color of dust.

"Sir?" Although he still maintained his smile, it was now hanging on his bony face like a wet shirt on a clothesline. "You are looking for something?" There was a faint trace of an accent to his voice. German, maybe? I didn't know. I opened my mouth to say something and nothing came out.

I stared at him as, with the help of a cane, he rose from his chair. Now the smile was almost entirely gone. I didn't think he recognized me. He wouldn't have had much reason to. The day we came to his stall, I'd left Lexi to peruse his wares while I went hunting for treasures among the stacks of old books on the opposite side of the market.

"You sold my wife a blanket," I said at last, the words like broken glass tumbling off my tongue. "A...a child's blanket."

"Yes, yes," he said, bracing one gnarled hand on the edge of the counter for support. He wasn't remembering Lexi, merely acknowledging that yes, indeed he sometimes sold people blankets.

Jesus Christ, I thought. *What are you doing here? He's just an old man. Just a regular old man selling off his children's ratty old clothes for some spare change.*

"I..." Though I had practiced them in my sleep and before the mirror, heard them echoing around my skull a hundred times prior to my coming here, the words would not come now that I was face to face with him. *It killed her,* I'd imagined telling him. *It killed her and I think you know that. I think you knew it would when you sold it to her.* Looking at him there, squinting at me in confusion, a threadbare old man in a threadbare old suit, I saw that I was wrong. I had vilified him because I needed a villain and in my despair, he was truly the only tangible, reachable one. Without him, I was left chasing ghosts or letting them chase me until there was no place left to hide but the grave.

I started to back away. "I'm sorry. I...I'm sorry."

"Wait, sir..."

I ignored his summons as I made my way back through the crowd, my mind in chaos. I had put everything on this moment. There were no cards left in my hand. Without him as the man with the answers, I was left hollow and defeated. I hurried back to the car, tears streaming down my face, ignoring the curious looks from the bargain hunters. Sweat trickled in cold rivulets down over my ribs. This was it. This was the end. Nowhere left to turn.

Three feet from the car, I remembered the blanket in the trunk.

That alone might not have been enough for me to change my mind about the course of action I was going to take, one that would end this nightmare forever—*home, drink, pills, eternal peace*—but the more I tried to shake it, the more a single question persisted. *How did he* not *know?*

Assuming I wasn't completely out of my mind with grief and imagining everything that had happened since Robin died, *how* would an old man have possession of that blanket and not know there was something wrong with it? There were, of course, any number of sane and logical responses to this question, foremost among them the possibility that Blanky was just a fucking blanket, after all. Another possibility was that, if there was indeed something supernatural about it, maybe the old man truly *didn't* know what he'd been selling us. Maybe it had never acted in a way that gave him pause. Maybe it had been *dormant* until it found itself with younger people to destroy, like an animal holing up for the winter until prey made itself available.

One hand on the car door handle, I decided there really was only one way to be sure about the old man.

I was going to have to reintroduce him to Blanky.

* * *

The afternoon grew late, the shadows long. The clouds behind the Chase building were the color of bruises as they chased down the sun. A breeze had risen. I could hear it whispering through the decorative evergreens surrounding the park even over the siren song from Agnes Obel on my car stereo.

It was quarter past five and the square was not nearly so full now. The mob had dispersed, leaving only stragglers behind, those tenacious few unwilling to go home without a prize. They wandered around like zombies, eyes narrowed as they scanned what little treasures remained. The food truck was gone now too, and most of the vendors were packing up their wares. They looked exhausted but satisfied, their pockets and lockboxes stuffed with cash from the horde of buyers seduced into purchasing things they didn't need, just as Lexi had been.

The old man was breaking down his stall. It was a deceptively simple process. Four walls, a roof, and a canopy, all of them disconnecting as easy as you please, like a hut made of Lego. The material looked cheap and flimsy, probably particle board, and in a matter of minutes, it lay in a pile at his feet. With the stall undone, I could see the car parked behind it. It was an old reddish-brown Dodge Dynasty, so rust-eaten and full of holes it looked as if a gunman had used it for target practice. The windows were opaque with dust, and the front bumper was held in place by a twisted wire hanger. The windshield was spider-webbed with cracks on the passenger side. A blue handicapped placard hung from the rearview mirror, which probably explained how he was still able to drive a vehicle that should long ago have been bent into steel origami at a wrecking yard. Into this monster, the old man dutifully fed his piles of baby clothes. He did not toss them in there as I had Blanky. No, he placed them in there with such tenderness they might have contained the babies for which the clothes had been made. Then he shut the trunk, dusted off his suit, looked around at nothing in particular, and got into his car, his work done for the day.

It took him a long time to start the engine. The handful of vendors still occupying the square jumped at the sound of gunfire and looked in the direction of the Dodge as it coughed out a cloud of dirty blue smoke the breeze carried straight into their faces. If the old man noticed, he offered no look of apology. He simply continued grinding the engine until it finally, begrudgingly caught.

When I saw him look out through the back window in order to safely guide the vehicle out of the square, I keyed the ignition. It started smoothly, the engine rumbling to life. Still, what little sound my car had made had clearly been enough to draw the attention of the vendors, all of whom turned as one to look at me.

There were ragged dark hollows where their faces should have been.

8

DRAWING UPON EVERY CRIME SHOW I had ever seen—Barney Miller would have been proud—I followed the old man home at a safe distance, keeping three or four cars between us on the highway at all times. It wasn't easy, though. The plume of smoke from his exhaust coupled with his penchant for pumping the brakes at odd intervals led almost every car to overtake him, many of them with vehicular exhortations of their displeasure. Thinking back on it, I'm not sure why I took such pains to ensure he didn't spot me. It's not like he knew my car, or would have noticed me behind the wheel. I guess I was just being cautious out of fear that he knew a lot more than he'd pretended, that it might behoove me to be wary of a man who could knowingly sell an instrument of murder to a pregnant woman.

Twilight fell as we left the city behind, the traffic narrowing along with the roads, and pretty soon, as Venus sparkled in the gloaming like a diamond on blue velvet, it was just me tailing the burning red lights of the old man's Dodge through roads enwombed by gnarled and leafless trees.

As I sailed through the encroaching dark, an awful loneliness crept over me as I recalled how many times I had driven this car with Lexi in the passenger seat laughing at some inane joke I'd made, or navigating with measured patience when the GPS failed us. I even missed having her there to argue with me. I'd have sold my soul to see her face twisted in rage, to feel her spittle on my cheek as she snapped at me over yet another instance of my insensitivity. All these moments, even the less pleasant ones, are snapshots we can never replace once they're lost, and it leaves us wishing for just the slightest glimpse of them if it means we can feel whole again. If it means we can pretend just for an instant that we're still alive.

But therein lay the problem, of course. They were gone. I was still alive. And without Robin and Lexi, that seemed like an impotent state, a redundancy that needed fixing, all those memories nothing more than piles of ash, or dirt, useless to me now.

Up ahead, the old man's turn signal flashed, and I eased my foot down on the brake, watched as he angled his rusted ruin onto an unpaved road that ran a quarter mile before turning again and vanishing into the woods.

I waited, certain now I knew where he, and by extension I, was going.

I had seen it in my dreams.

What I didn't yet know was whether he would be alone, or if the woman would be there too.

Only when the trees quenched his headlights did I follow.

* * *

Eventually the road became a trail which, though it had clearly been traversed by vehicles, didn't seem intended for them. Thick twisted roots rose from the dirt to scrape at the underside of the car even as low hanging branches rapped their knuckles against the roof. Brambles and shrubs crowded me on both sides until it felt like I was driving not through nature but an angry crowd that might at any moment tear me free of it. The uneven terrain jostled me in my seat, making my teeth crack together. It was hard to keep my hands on the wheel and the car on the road. Animals fled so quickly through my headlights, I couldn't tell what kind they were.

I lost track of how much time passed, felt disorientated by the sudden dark and the inefficacy of my highbeams to keep it at bay. The car was now cocooned in branches that made tortured shrieking sounds against the metal until my fillings ached. I thought I saw phosphorescent lights in the distance, but it was only lightning bugs rising before the windshield. Other lights glowed in pairs as nocturnal animals watched my progress from the safety of the woods. A sudden splat as a wet leaf hit my windshield and I had to swallow the urge to scream.

The longer it went on, the more I began to think that it might never end, that maybe this was the trap in which the woman wished to keep me. Her endgame, infinitely cruel in its banality. I'd expected a showdown which would ultimately end in my death, a death I would not resist once I'd uncovered the reason for it all. The notion that I might be trapped for eternity with my ghosts seemed like the worst kind of hell.

I rolled down the windows. I don't know why. Perhaps it was because I was baking alive in the heat of my own panic. Perhaps I felt like I was about to pass out. Or maybe I just wanted to let loose the scream that seemed to perpetually be surging up my throat. But I opened it and the branches, now not branches at all but impossibly long and wet clambering fingers, exploded into the car to find me. And find me they did, probing their sticky fingers into my eyes and mouth. I let go of the wheel and clutched at them, but they were too slick, too fast, and whipped away only to lash back at me and score the flesh of my face.

I screamed.

I screamed.

I flailed at them.

When the car veered off the road, I didn't care, didn't know.

As the world tumbled and turned, I could only struggle and yank and tear and bat at the branches, the tendrils, the boneless arms with their verdant baby fingers as they tried to infiltrate my throat and prod the soft flesh of my eyelids, pulling them away so they could slip inside.

Then the car met sudden resistance, the world slammed to a halt, and the mass of branches withdrew like a hand burned by a flame, content to let the darkness take its place.

* * *

She turns her head at the sound from the woods. It may as well be

61

the horn signaling the imminent arrival of the invaders. Soon the night will be lit by the glow of their lamps and their torches, and yet again, they will come to fall at her feet. She raises a hand and bends a forefinger. The dolls follow her instruction, gathering in a perfect circle amid the symbols on the floor.

They look up at her, their faces falling to pieces like shattered porcelain, revealing the depthless hollows within. Stars swirl and universes ignite within that cavernous cosmic dark. There is a low hum in the room, a mumbling that comes from nowhere and everywhere at once.

The woman leans forward, her spine making the sound of shells breaking in a gloved hand as it reshapes to accommodate the motion. She brushes aside the thatched mass of her writhing hair and brings her face close to the dolls. She can feel the cold from them. Lightless, amorphous tendrils spindle outward from the hollows, umbilically uniting the children to one another and then to her like spokes from a burned wheel. Only once they are connected does she feed them what they need.

It is, as always, a story, but not one they have heard before.

This one is about a man who didn't know how to love his wife and child enough so the gods made him pay for his apathy by taking them away.

The children listen intently until the sound of dead leaves being crushed underfoot brings their attention to the warped cabin door.

9

THERE WAS A RED FLICKER IN MY RIGHT EYE as I stumbled toward the cabin. My vision jolted with every labored step, and my breathing sounded like someone raking leaves. There was so much pain in so many places, I couldn't identify any of them. Distantly, I wondered if something was broken. I couldn't quite tell if I was even awake, or if any of what I was seeing was real. I vaguely recalled waking up upside down, still strapped into the driver seat of my car. A tree branch had punched a hole in the windshield, the sheared off end of it like the tip of a spear before my right eye. That I still had my life was a miracle. That I hadn't been blinded was even more of one.

After crawling free of the wreck, I'd walked aimlessly, hoping I'd eventually find myself back on the trail, back on the road. I wanted to go home, wanted to wake up in my own bed to find Lexi lying next to me, and Robin safe in her crib. I wanted all the horror undone, and in my confusion, head throbbing mercilessly, I demanded to know why it couldn't be so. Because it wasn't fair, any of it. I had done nothing to deserve such a callous intervention of fate and was no longer content to accept it as reality.

I stumbled along for what felt like hours before I realized I was holding Blanky in my right hand. It was caked in mud and leaves, and perhaps it was only the breeze or my own crippled vision, but it appeared to be moving. I could feel the material brushing against my bloody fingers as if it was not a blanket at all but a pillowcase filled with eels. When I raised my head and saw the soft amber glow of lights ahead of us, I figured I'd imagined nothing and maybe the thing was just excited to be home.

The old man. I'd been following the old man.

I had to keep reminding myself why I was here, what had happened to me to leave me broken and bleeding on this path in the middle of nowhere. It was difficult. What little reason I had left demanded I turn around and try to find the highway, to flag down a passing car and go straight to the hospital, or at the very least, home where I belonged. This was madness, it said, and I would not find whatever it was I had come here to seek. It would only end in misery.

Blanky coiled itself around my wrist like a snake, the baby teeth in the hem digging into the flesh of my wrist.

It seemed my destination was not up for debate, so I moved on toward the cabin lights, every step sending a bolt of agony through me.

* * *

I don't know what I expected to see once that door opened. Hell itself? The tall woman bent almost double, gnarled hands pulling me inside while the swirling vortex in her face rid me of the last of my sanity? Would there be children pretending to be dolls seated on the floor, baby fingers poking from their eyes to wave perversely at me in the moments before my life was extinguished? Would Robin be among them? Would I see someone nailed to the floorboards, eyes wide with the panic only those of us in the final moments of our existences truly know? I felt the fear and the grim acceptance of such things warring within me, but was no longer in any condition to retreat, should it even have presented itself as an option. Instead, after knocking a single time, I simply stood a few feet from the door, weaving on my feet, all but blind in one eye, my chest feeling like broken glass, and waited.

At length, I saw a shadow move behind the curtains of the low-slung cabin. Heard footsteps from within. Felt a strange warmth flood my body. Not quite calm, but close.

The door opened and a face hove into view.

"Yes?"

He was still wearing the threadbare suit pants, but had discarded the rest in favor of a raggedy white T-shirt with old sweat stains beneath the armpits. The hat was gone too, revealing a pate threaded with scars. His arms were rail-thin and speckled with freckles and liver spots. The old man peered warily at me through his spectacles, glass eye lost in darkness.

"I'm here," I said.

He frowned as he inspected me, wariness turning to alarmed recognition. "You. I saw you today. Why…what happened to you? Do you need the police? You're hurt."

"Accident," I mumbled. "But you know why I'm here."

With great effort, I summoned enough focus to take in the room behind him. I can admit now to a certain disappointment at the sight of it, because it was just a room. There was no witch, no dolls, no man staked to the floor, no symbols carved into the wood. Instead, there was a tattered floral-pattered sofa, a sheepskin rug, and an old portable TV on a stand. The smell of popcorn and butter told me all I needed to know about the insidious activities I'd intruded upon. The old man had been preparing to watch a movie.

This was not The Other Place. It was just a house.

"Do you have a phone?" he asked, shaking me gently by the shoulder, indicating it wasn't the first time he'd posed the question. I looked squarely at him, saw the slight trace of unease in his good eye. He should have been afraid. I had no business being here, and I was not myself. It's not usual these days to find someone who would open the door to a stranger covered in blood. Most people would call the cops first. Of course, he didn't have a phone or maybe that's exactly what he'd have done.

"Mister? Sir?" He shook me harder. "Do you have a phone with you?"

"Back in the car," I told him, "Or, it was. I don't know."

"You should come in and sit down."

He moved away from me, one hand extended, inviting me into his sanctuary.

I didn't move. "Is this your home?"

He squinted at me. "This? Oh no. I just use it sometimes when

I work in Columbus. Saves me a long trip home. It belongs to my brother, or it used to. He's passed now."

The accent, faint but there. He came from somewhere in Europe.

"You don't share it with anyone?"

He lowered his arm, clearly content to answer but worried that the questions were coming to him courtesy of a concussion. "I used to share it with my wife. She's no longer with us either."

No longer with us.

I smiled at that. Lexi. Robin. No longer with us, as if they'd simply left the room.

Frowning, the old man looked down at my hand and saw the blanket. Saw Blanky. I saw him see it and watched him as carefully as my juddering vision would allow. The blanket tightened under his scrutiny. Recognition?

"You should use that to stop the bleeding," he said, but he looked confused. "Did I...?"

"Did you sell that to my wife? Yes, you did."

Concern became suspicion now and he took a single step backward, one hand reaching for the door. I stepped inside, over the threshold. To shut me out, he'd have to hit me with the door and he didn't look inclined to do that to an injured man.

"Why is it here?" he asked me, a note of fear in his voice. "I mean, why do you have it with you?"

"Do you know what it is? Do you know what it does? You do, don't you?"

He moved back another step. I took a corresponding step forward and elbowed the door shut behind me.

"It's a blanket. I don't understand what you—"

"You killed my wife and my baby girl." It sounded like I might be crying, but I couldn't be sure. "You sold this to my wife and it killed them both. I need you to tell me how you could do that to them. To me."

There was nothing but naked fear on the old man's face now. He looked around the room as if trying to register an escape route or the whereabouts of the nearest weapon. He held his arms out to his sides as if considering actual flight. "Sir...I am not sure what you're talking about, but I think you should sit down. I think you, maybe, hurt your head. I can go to the cabin up the road and see if they can call for help, or maybe we can look for your phone."

I closed in on him, Blanky so tight around my hand it was cutting off the circulation. "Did she threaten you, the witch? Did she make you do it? Did she kill your wife to show she was serious? Did you wake up one morning to find this blanket stuffed into her throat? Please tell me you had no other choice or I don't know what I'll do."

He backed further away into the room but did not take his eyes off me. There was a small kitchenette at the back of the cabin. If he made it there, he'd probably find a knife and end me. I had to make him answer.

"Just tell me, please. I'm begging you. Tell me why you sold this blanket to Lexi."

His brow was sheened with sweat. He licked his lips, good eye flicking from the walls to the floor to my face, and when at last he spoke, it was with a nervous tremor in his voice. "I gave that blanket to your wife because she...she asked me to. She wanted it. I didn't even take her money. I told her she could have it as a gift. A gift to...to celebrate her first child."

I stared at him, searching his face for the lie, for the cleverly concealed truth behind his claim. I stared for a very long time, until the doubt returned and the strength of my convictions began to leave me.

"I...I don't know why I'm here. Please...help me."

But then, just for a moment, I saw his face start to swim, saw the edges becomes less clear, less defined, saw the flare of blazing stars beneath his skin like red suns seen through a veil.

Still wearing the mask of fake sincerity, he said, "I'm very sorry for your loss," and I was jerked forward by the blanket in my hand hard enough to crack my neck.

We were on the floor then, me straddling him as he struggled against me, looking down as Blanky shattered the old man's dentures on its way into his mouth, forcing him to swallow them.

The blanket took my fist down with it and thus I felt the warmth of his throat as it tried to resist the obstruction while still struggling to draw air. Air hissed in through his flaring nostrils, tears streamed from his eye. He looked up at me in absolute horror, hands clenched on my arm, trying to force me away. Part of me was glad that he now knew what horror was, the same horror in which he had been complicit for decades, perhaps longer. Blanky surged forward and I found myself assisting, putting all my weight behind it until the life left the old man's eyes and his body stopped bucking. I smelled shit and piss as his body let go and I rolled away from him, my head spinning. The stars continued to dance before my eyes as I rose to my feet, exhausted now. I stood looking at the body for the longest time, not convinced that an agent of supernatural forces might not just cough the blanket out and come back to life, perhaps with vengeance in mind.

But he didn't. He lay there, dead amid the foulness of his own excreta, mouth open, throat swollen with the child's blanket. He hadn't given me the answers I'd come here to get. He'd lied, content to remain a coward rather than give me the peace I needed. But that was fine. He was dead, punished for his part in the horror show, unable to visit his evil upon anybody else, and that would have to suffice, at least until the woman finally decided to show herself.

Before I left, I caught a glimpse of myself in the darkened window above the kitchen sink. My face was gone, in its place, a hole through which I could see the night beyond.

* * *

I don't know how I got home or how many times I collapsed before I got there, but the sun had risen in a sky that looked suddenly alien to me when I finally turned the corner into my development.

The police were there, two cruisers parked outside my door, four officers milling around talking. Harriet and Tony Dean were there too. Of course they were, always so eager to be involved in other people's lives. They gasped in horror when they saw me. The policemen's hands strayed to their holsters as if I'd inadvertently wandered onto a Western movie set at high noon.

"What's going on?" I asked, offering a smile to calm their nerves, because they looked as if they'd seen a ghost. I must assume I looked like one.

Two of the officers approached me, grim determination on their faces. "Mr. Brannigan?"

I tried to say something to them, to raise my bloody hands to show them I meant no harm, but then the world tilted and spun away from me and I was gone, their voices trailing me down into the dark.

10

I AWOKE IN A HOSPITAL BED, my right foot and right arm in a cast, my skull swaddled in bandages. Harsh daylight burned through the pristine white blinds. A pulse monitor had been cinched like a futuristic clothes peg over my finger. A female police officer sat next to the bed. I recognized her from the night Lexi died. The woman I'd offended in my grief. At the foot of the bed stood a large black man in a suit. His gaze was not kind. He introduced himself as Detective Marshall Murray from the Columbus Police Department. He asked me if I felt up to answering some questions. I told him I was, which was a lie, and at some point, I faded out. When I woke up it was night time and I was alone but for the solemn beeping of machines, and I had been handcuffed to the bed rail.

I slept, and did not dream. It was a small mercy.

Eventually, the detective returned and he had even less patience than before.

He asked me for my version of events starting all the way back to the night Robin had died.

So, I told him, and then he told me the version of events *he* believed to be true, and it differed greatly from mine. Still, I did not protest as he painted a picture of a soulless murderer, a heartless monster. I just let him talk.

"You can of course call your attorney to be present with you while we do this. In fact, I'd recommend it at this point," he told me, but I declined. I might have countered that I had nothing to hide, except, if I gave his story more credence than my own, it appeared I'd been hiding a lot.

My neighbors, the Deans, had been busy, it seemed.

They told the police I'd been drinking a lot in the days leading up to Robin's death, that I'd been frustrated with the restrictions put on me by an unplanned child who never stopped crying, that exhaustion had started making me seem a little off. Said they heard our fights through the walls. I was short-tempered, haggard, irritable. I'd lost weight, and although nobody thought that I would ever intentionally kill my own child, well, given all that had happened since, wasn't it the most reasonable assumption? Worse, they claimed that the night I went to try and save Lexi, I didn't tell them to call the police as I raced to my car. They said I was enraged and drunk and threatening to "make that fucking bitch sorry she ever left me." They say *that's* why they called the police.

I must admit, that doesn't sound at all like me, but then, how many times have I written in this very narrative that I didn't feel like myself. From seven years of being with Lexi, I knew her parents liked to retire early for the evening. I knew that they were heavy sleepers. I also knew where they left the spare key. I suppose it's not entirely far-fetched to think that a grief-ridden husband addled by drink might want to take his frustration out on the woman who abandoned him to his suffering. Maybe if I'd received a video that night of her choking to death on Blanky, I could have gotten myself off the hook. But there's no video. Just a record of her call. Even if there had been a video, I guess I could have filmed it myself. It's truly amazing how distorted events can seem through other people's eyes.

And then of course, there's the old man.

One of the first questions they asked me when I regained consciousness was where I had been all night. Marcy had seen me load the blanket into the trunk, had seen me stalking out to my car. Worried that they were now living next door to a murderer or a madman, they'd called the police on me again. When I showed up covered in blood, well, that did nothing to dissuade anyone.

So I told them I went to see the old man from the market and that I knew he had killed my wife and child by selling us a cursed blanket so I went to make him answer for it, and when he wouldn't, I gave him a taste of his own medicine. Despite the seriousness of the matter and the sincerity in my voice, I couldn't restrain a laugh at how ridiculous it all sounded when I said it out loud. The looks on the faces of the detective and his fellow officers only heightened the hilarity for me.

I was the only one amused.

* * *

When I was back on my feet, they took my shoes and my fingerprints, and sent me to jail.

* * *

For the record, I don't believe their version of events. I may have lost my mind for a time, but grief makes everyone crazy. Losing someone makes you lose yourself, makes you yearn for the impossible: one more day with the lost, an end to the pain, a cure for the spiritual malaise that eats you alive every morning you wake up alone. It makes you believe in wishes and other places. In suicide.

I believe I did the right thing. I know I loved my wife and baby daughter. Yes, she cried a lot; yes, Lexi left me when I needed her, but I loved them and would never have hurt them, even if I never really knew how to be a father, or a good husband, but I'm hardly alone in that. Turn on the TV any day of the week and you'll see countless examples of people who should be locked away for the sake of their loved ones.

The world is full of evil.

I'm not that person.

My time spent here, caged in a cold dank cell alone with my thoughts, has only bolstered my belief in other worlds and the things that exist there. I have come to think of it as the ultimate escape, and I no longer fear it.

I've been having the dreams again. They're much more vivid than before.

So tonight, I expect to hear a soft whisper against the bars as Blanky comes to find me from wherever the police have it stored. I imagine I will feel the warmth of it as it crawls up my chest, those teeth pressed against my lips as it forces them open. I will embrace the temporary agony as it the dirty cotton fills my throat, and then...

And then I imagine I will find myself *there*, with *her*, down on my knees before the witch who was never a witch at all, but The Goddess of Grief, my face upraised as my false façade shatters in pieces to the floor, exposing the hollow that has tormented me my whole life. There will be no blame there, no judgment, only love.

Because I may not always know who I am, but she does.

* * *

MURDER SUSPECT FOUND MISSING IN CELL

By Geraldine Archer
The Columbus Dispatch

Posted at 2.36 p.m.
Updated at 5.22 p.m.

In a scene better suited to a Hollywood movie, triple homicide suspect Steven Brannigan was found missing from his cell at the Tri-County Regional Jail in Mechanicsburg, Ohio in the early hours of this morning. Brannigan had been awaiting trial for the murders of his 11-month old daughter, his wife, and a retired professor. According to one of the attending officers, who spoke on condition of anonymity, there was no obvious sign of the method Brannigan used to escape. The doors were locked and there were no structural faults within the cell that could have been exploited. It remains, he said, "an absolute puzzle." The administration is currently

73

considering the possibility that Brannigan worked with a staff member inside the jail to facilitate his escape. Adding to the mystery are the only clues found at the scene: a sixty-page document handwritten by Brannigan in which he details an alternate version of the events of which he stands accused, the stub of a pencil, and a single baby's tooth. Authorities maintain Brannigan must have smuggled the tooth in with him, as, according to our source, there is "no other earthly reason for it to be there."

ABOUT THE AUTHOR

Born and raised in a small harbor town in the south of Ireland, Kealan Patrick Burke knew from a very early age that he was going to be a horror writer. The combination of an ancient locale, a horror-loving mother, and a family full of storytellers, made it inevitable that he would end up telling stories for a living. Since those formative years, he has written five novels, over a hundred short stories, six collections, and edited four acclaimed anthologies. In 2004, he was honored with the Bram Stoker Award for his novella *The Turtle Boy.*

Kealan has worked as a waiter, a drama teacher, a mapmaker, a security guard, an assembly-line worker at Apple Computers, a salesman (for a day), a bartender, landscape gardener, vocalist in a grunge band, curriculum content editor, fiction editor at Gothic.net, and, most recently, a fraud investigator.

When not writing, Kealan designs book covers through his company Elderlemon Design.

A number of his books have been optioned for film.

Visit him on the web at www.kealanpatrickburke.com

Made in the USA
San Bernardino, CA
25 May 2019